"Your father left us in joint command."

Griff spoke persuasively. "Can't we work together, Trina — for the good of the firm?"

"You cared a lot about the good of the firm when you deserted Compson's, didn't you?"

"At least I learned how to run a business. What do you know about it?"

"I grew up here," Trina said shortly. "The glassworks has been part of my life since I was a child. And let me tell you something else, Griff Tyzak: Compson's still belongs to *me.* I have the final say in its affairs, and if you can't accept that, go back to your studio and those monstrosities you call art. We managed without you once before, and I for one would be happy to do it again!"

Books by Nicola West

HARLEQUIN ROMANCES
2526—DEVIL'S GOLD
2592—NO ROOM IN HIS LIFE
2610—WILDTRACK
2640—THE TYZAK INHERITANCE

HARLEQUIN PRESENTS
589—LUCIFER'S BRAND

These books may be available at your local bookseller.

For a list of all titles currently available,
send your name and address to:

Harlequin Reader Service
P.O. Box 52040, Phoenix, AZ 85072-2040
Canadian address: P.O. Box 2800, Postal Station A,
5170 Yonge St., Willowdale, Ont. M2N 5T5

The Tyzak Inheritance

Nicola West

Harlequin Books

TORONTO • NEW YORK • LONDON
AMSTERDAM • PARIS • SYDNEY • HAMBURG
STOCKHOLM • ATHENS • TOKYO • MILAN

Original hardcover edition published in 1983
by Mills & Boon Limited

ISBN 0-373-02640-4

Harlequin Romance first edition August 1984

With grateful thanks to Stuart Crystal
and especially to
Christopher Stuart
who was so helpful in the writing
of this book

———————◆———————

CHAPTER ONE

'Griff Tyzak?' There was real horror in Trina's voice as she stared at the lawyer and repeated his words. 'Griff Tyzak is to share responsibility for Compson Crystal with *me*? You can't mean it! There has to be some mistake.'

Ambrose Henry shook his head. He looked uncomfortable – had been ever since he had first approached Trina, on the day of her father's funeral, and asked if he could come to see her the next day to talk over the will. 'I never like the old-fashioned method of reading the will after the ceremony,' he had observed. 'Much better to discuss it quietly on a – well, let's say a less emotional occasion. Perhaps I could call tomorrow morning – say about eleven?'

'Yes, of course,' Trina replied, wondering why he looked so ill at ease. He and her father had been friends and colleagues for years, of course, and he must have been sorry for William Compson's death at only sixty-five. But she sensed that the lawyer's discomfort was due to more than that—though what it could be, she simply couldn't imagine. Her father's will must be straightforward enough—she was the main beneficiary, there being no other children or close members of the family, and she had always understood that she would take over the glassworks in Stourbridge when the time came. She was perfectly capable of doing so, after all.

But now it seemed that her father had had other ideas. Ideas that were so unexpected and so disturbing that she couldn't really take them in.

'I don't understand,' she said, getting up and walking restlessly up and down the room. She had asked Ambrose Henry into the library, which had been her father's favourite room, and she roamed unseeingly between the shelves, pausing by the tall windows.

Outside was the bleakness of winter, the trees bare against the heavy grey of the sky, the ground hard and frozen. The library fire burned cheerfully behind her, but for once its flames, their red-gold colour glinting on her smooth cap of blonde hair, did nothing to warm her heart.

'Dad hadn't even *seen* Griff for years,' she went on, turning away from the window and looking full at the lawyer. 'Why should he do such a thing? After the way Griff treated him—it's just beyond understanding! I can't believe he meant it.'

'I'm afraid there's no question about that. He was most careful about the wording—it's all quite plain.' Ambrose hesitated. 'I did suggest that he should at least tell you of his intentions, but he evidently didn't take that advice.'

'He certainly did not!' Again Trina set off on an aimless tour of the library. She stopped and poked restlessly at the fire. Her emotions were confused, a welter of conflicting feeling. How *could* her father have done this to her? What possible reason could he have? If only she could feel angry with him, she thought miserably—but she had seldom felt angry with her father and she couldn't start now that he was dead.

'When was the will drawn up?' she asked. 'When Griff was still here? Surely it could be contested——'

But Ambrose was shaking his head. 'The will was quite recently updated,' he told her. 'A few minor bequests added, that kind of thing. . . . The clause about Mr Tyzak had been in for some time, it's true, but there was no question of it being removed.' He paused, then went on gently: 'It wouldn't really do to contest it, you know. For one thing, I doubt if you would win any action—many courts might take the view that it was a sensible provision to make, in view of your youth and Mr Tyzak's experience——'

'And the fact that I'm a woman, I suppose!' Trina cut in bitterly. 'But I'm not exactly a teenager, Ambrose—I'm twenty-five and quite experienced in the glass trade. I've grown up with it, for goodness' sake! If Dad thought I needed the help of a more experienced man, why didn't he pick on Robert Nicklin? He's been right through the factory from an apprentice and now he's Works Director—wouldn't he have been the ideal choice?' Her voice shook as she thought of sharing the managing directorship with Griff Tyzak. She wouldn't do it—she *couldn't*! There had to be some way out.

'You'll have Robert Nicklin's help on the Board as it is,' Ambrose pointed out. 'As well as the other members. No, I'm sure your father had his own very good reasons for what he did. And think of the publicity that would result from any attempt to have the clause overthrown. Unpleasant publicity, doing no good either to your father's name or to that of the firm.'

Trina stared at him, then turned away. He was quite right, of course. Publicity of that kind would do the firm no good at all, either in the public view or among the workers themselves—men who had known her father all their working lives, men she had grown up among, whose families had worked for Compson Crystal ever since it was founded over a hundred years ago.

'So what do I do?' she asked dully. 'Let Griff Tyzak just walk in and take over? See him betray us again, as he's already betrayed us once?' A thought struck her and she whipped round, staring at the lawyer with accusing eyes. 'Is that why he turned up at the funeral? Did he already know about this? *Did he?*'

The lawyer raised his hand. 'No, no—at least, not from me. I don't know if I've ever even spoken to him—I hadn't seen him for several years. But I would have thought that your father would have discussed it with him—it means a considerable amount of responsibility for him, after all, and one which he might not have been prepared to accept.'

'Oh, he'd accept it all right,' Trina declared bitterly. 'What I don't understand is why Dad—oh, well, there's no use in going over all that again. But you're right, Ambrose—he must have known about it. He asked if he could come to see me here.'

'Well, no doubt everything will become clear then.' The lawyer rose to his feet. 'I'm afraid I have to go now, Katrina—another appointment. I'll leave this copy of the will for you to go through at your leisure. Don't hesitate to call me if there's anything at all you don't understand. And perhaps I could call in again in a few days for another discussion. I expect there'll be things you'll need to talk about.'

'I'm sure there will,' Trina agreed grimly as she saw him out. 'But I doubt if seeing Griff Tyzak will make things much clearer. He's deviousness itself, that man— I just can't imagine how Dad could have thought we'd ever be able to work together. But perhaps he'll be more of a sleeping M.D.—he's got his own studio, after all.'

'And making a very good name for himself,' Ambrose agreed. 'I don't think you've too much to worry about, my dear. As you say, that will almost certainly continue to be his main interest.'

Trina nodded and smiled as she let him out of the front door. But her face as she made her way back to the library was thoughtful. She wasn't at all sure that Griff Tyzak would be content to leave the running of Compson Crystal to her, even though it was her family's firm. As she remembered him, he wasn't the type to leave anything to anyone else. He'd always wanted to have a finger in all the pies—and running his own glass studio for ten years wasn't likely to have changed that!

She thought back to that moment at the funeral yesterday when she had glanced up from the graveside and seen him standing there, his thick black hair whipped around his face by the wind that tore across the hillside. The sight of him had gone through her body with a jolt—what was *he* doing here? she had wondered resentfully. It was years since he had been near her father, at least as far as she knew, though it seemed now as if she might be wrong about that. At all events, her father had never mentioned seeing him, had spoken little about him since the day Griff had left the factory where he had learned all he knew and set up his own studio. Trina had been bewildered then and she was bewildered still. They had *needed* Griff Tyzak—he was, without doubt, the most talented glassmaker they had had for years, and he had been at the peak of his powers when he had left them. And although they had trained some very highly-skilled men since, none of them had ever quite matched the flair that Griff had shown.

Trina had said this to her father once, making it quite plain what she thought of Griff's defection. But William Compson had merely smiled and remarked that every man had a right to fulfil his own potential in the way he thought best. 'Griff has a very unusual talent,' he told her. 'He needs to express it freely. Staying here might have held him back.' He had given her a sideways glance and added: 'Perhaps your feelings are a little mixed, Trina. After all, you always rather liked Griff, didn't you?'

And Trina had felt the hot blush colour her cheeks and turned away from that too-perceptive glance. Yes, she *had* liked Griff. And there had been a few times when she had caught a look of equal interest in Griff's velvet-brown eyes as he looked up from his work to find her watching him. Perhaps that was why his decision to leave the factory had affected her so deeply. She had taken it as a personal rejection as well.

But that didn't apply any more. She was older now—ten years older. She was no longer a spectator at the factory but an important part of it. As chief designer, she had considerable say not only in the design of the glassware but in packaging, display and advertising. Surely her word would carry more weight than that of an outsider, even if he had served his apprenticeship in the glassworks and continued to work there for several years.

He must have known the provisions of her father's will, though. Otherwise why come to the funeral—and why ask to see her later? A shudder ran through her body as she recalled the way he had approached her, his easy, loping stride all too familiar from the days when she had hung around the factory just in the hope of seeing him walk by. She hadn't watched with adoration this time, though. Her face had been set and cold as he came closer.

He had held out his hand, but Trina ignored it, turning away slightly as if she hadn't seen it. With a faint shrug, he put it back into his coat pocket and stood looking down at her so that she had to tilt her head to meet his eyes. He looked older, she thought irrelevantly, his face thinner, almost gaunt in the harsh wind. But there was a strength there that had been only hinted at in his earlier days. His jaw was firm, his mouth uncompromising. He wouldn't be an easy man to cross.

'I just wanted to say I'm sorry, Trina,' he said quietly. 'About your father. He was a fine man.'

'You should know,' she retorted. 'He helped you enough.'

Griff inclined his head. 'He did indeed. And I've never stopped feeling grateful for the start he gave me and for his encouragement.'

'You've an odd way of showing it, then!' she flashed, only dimly aware of the other people who were now moving away from the graveside. 'Leaving us like that—setting up your own studio——'

'It's not such an unusual thing to happen, Trina. And I worked a good few years after my apprenticeship——'

'We needed your skills,' she reminded him coldly. 'You knew that perfectly well. Yet you still went.'

Griff sighed and brushed back the dark hair that blew around his lean face. 'Look, Trina,' he said, 'this is neither the time nor the place for us to argue. And I don't want to quarrel with you, anyway. We used to get along so well.' He paused for a moment. 'Can I come and see you some time soon? To have a talk?'

'We've nothing to talk about, that I know of.'

'Well, if not then it won't take long, will it? But I think you'll find we have. When would suit you, Trina?'

She wanted to say that no time would suit her, but

she knew that if Griff was determined to come, come he would. It might be just as well to get it over, and then perhaps she need never see him again. She shivered in a gust of icy wind and drew her dark grey cape closely around her.

'Make an appointment with Jean some time next week,' she said coolly, thinking how odd it was that Jean was now her secretary instead of her father's. But Griff shook his head.

'I'd rather come out to Compson House, if you don't mind. Would tomorrow be too soon? I'm staying up here for two or three days.'

'And how are they managing without you at the studio?' she enquired sarcastically. 'Can they cope for several days without the guiding force?'

'I employ artists and craftsmen,' he told her quietly. 'They don't need me breathing down their necks all the time. Well, Trina? Tomorrow, or would the next day be better for you?'

Suddenly she wanted nothing more than to get rid of him. People were waiting at the churchyard gate, watching curiously as she stood with this man from the past. She shrugged impatiently, as if it couldn't matter less when he came.

'Oh, any time will do. It doesn't matter.' And she turned and walked quickly away from him to the people she knew and felt safe with, the people she had grown up among. Her heart was beating fast and her skin prickled as if she had just escaped from some unspecified danger. But even as the idea came into her head she dismissed it angrily. What possible danger could Griff Tyzak be to her? He was nothing but a nuisance—and the sooner he went back to his studio in Herefordshire the better!

Finding herself once again staring out of the library window, Trina turned and flung herself into one of the deep armchairs. It was clear enough now why Griff Tyzak had approached her in the churchyard, and why he wanted to talk to her. He must have known all along about her father's will. How he must be gloating now, at the thought of Compson Crystal under his command! He probably expected her to be *glad* to have his experience and advice to help her with her new responsibilities. Well, he would soon find out his mistake there! She intended to leave him in no doubt as to her own feelings in the matter.

Gazing into the fire, she wondered again just why her father had made that condition. Ambrose Henry had explained it to her very carefully. Her inheritance of the shares, ensuring her place as Managing Director, was to come to her only on her acceptance of Griff Tyzak to share the position. Both appointments would have to be confirmed by a shareholders' meeting, of course, but he was convinced there would be no problem there. Trina's position was assured because of her ownership of a majority of shares, and Griff's would be accepted on the strength of his undoubted skills, his experience in running his own glass studio, and the fact that William Compson had wanted him there. Nobody was going to vote against that.

It looked as if, like it or not, she was going to have to accept the position. But that didn't mean she had to like it, or that she had to kowtow to the man she still believed had deserted the firm and her father just when he was most needed. No—her authority was at least as great as his, and she had the advantage of being on the spot, a part of the factory—and an important part, too. If Griff Tyzak thought he was going to come in and run things all his own way, he was very much mistaken!

Trina raised her head and looked thoughtfully round the room. Compson House was hers now, as was everything in it. She had grown up here, taking it all very much for granted, not taking much notice when the roof needed repair or the walls repointing. Now it was her responsibility—this house which had been built by her great-grandfather, old Joshua Compson, who had bought the glass factory when it was failing and built it up again. He had been an ironmaster, with works in nearby Wolverley, and Compson House had been built with the money made from iron. The

Compson family had lived there ever since, their lives shaped by the red sandstone of their home, the long views into Shropshire seen from the windows, and the glass factory that had, through the years, increased its reputation until today it was producing some of the finest tableware in the country—if not the world. And it had all come to her—Katrina Compson, the last of the line. From now on, the onus was on her.

She was startled out of her thoughts by a tap on the door. Mrs Aston, the housekeeper, looked round it, her face clearing when she saw Trina.

'Oh, there you are, miss. There's a visitor for you. I told him I didn't know if you were in—I thought you might not want to be disturbed.' She hesitated, but Trina knew already who the visitor must be and her heart kicked as she answered, thankful that her voice wasn't betraying her agitation.

'It's all right, Mrs Aston. I expect it's Mr Tyzak, isn't it? I've been expecting him to come some time.' And that doesn't say he's welcome and it doesn't say he's not, she thought, standing up, still conscious of a jumping heart and a sudden discomfort in her breathing. She bit her lip and tried to breathe slowly and deeply, as if she were going on stage. He mustn't see that she was nervous—that would be fatal. He must never, never know how he affected her.

Play it cool, that was the only way. However angry he made her, she must keep her temper. And she prayed that she'd be able to do so.

Griff Tyzak came into the room like a gust of fresh air. He was huge in a thick sheepskin coat, its collar turned up against the icy wind outside, his hands thrust deep into the pockets. Black hair lay blown across his forehead and he pushed it back from his face with a movement that spoke of hidden energy. His dark eyes glinted as he surveyed Trina, who felt suddenly small and defenceless in the face of so much dynamic power. But she held her ground and tilted her chin as she looked up at him, her green eyes matching his for glitter.

'You wanted to see me?' she enquired politely, hoping that the rapid beating of her heart wouldn't make her voice tremble.

'That was the general idea.' He paused, seeming oddly at a loss. His voice sent a thrill of unease through her; deep and velvety, it could be harsh and uncompromising too, she was sure, and for the first time she wondered if she would be able to stand out against him when their views clashed, as surely they must. He shrugged out of his coat and threw it on one of the armchairs, and her eyes moved over him, noting the broad shoulders under the thick sweater, the depth of his chest. She'd seen that chest and those shoulders naked in the heat of the glasshouse as he wielded the blowing-iron and produced some beautifully-shaped glass object—a decanter, perhaps, or a bowl —from the lump of glowing molten 'metal' brought from the furnace. He'd been the same as the other men then, dressed in rough working clothes, yet even so something had set him apart—something in his bearing, his quiet confidence in the skill he had developed from a combination of artistry and sheer hard work. He had been proud, and deserved to be.

'How are you, Trina?' he asked, his face grave as he looked down at her. 'It's a long time since we've talked.'

'And whose fault's that?' she flashed, already forgetting her resolutions to keep her temper.

Griff sighed. 'I know. It's all my fault—or so you believe. Well, we'll leave it at that, shall we? It's the future that's important now, not the past.'

'The future is part of the past. It's shaped by the past—you can't separate them.'

'Not entirely, perhaps. But you can't look back all your life, Trina. You have to build—take the good parts and use them as a foundation——'

'And the bad parts?'

He sighed and ran his fingers through his hair. 'Look, this will get us nowhere. I've told you, Trina, I had a great regard for your father. I've never forgotten the way he took me on and gave me my start. I'd like to repay that debt.'

'You could have done that by staying on here!'

'No—that's not true. But you're not in a mood to understand that, are you, Trina? Not even if I explained it to you step by step. So let's forget it, shall we, and start from where we are now?' His eyes narrowed as he looked at her. 'Agreed?'

'If you like,' she said stiffly. Griff waited a moment or two, then spoke again.

'So here we go. How are you, Trina? Nice to see you after all this time.' Trina said nothing and he went on: 'Now you say, "How are *you*, Griff? Yes, it is nice, isn't it? I've missed you around the gl——"'

'Oh, stop it!' Trina whipped away from him and stepped quickly to the window. 'You're just making fun—mocking—and it's all false and artificial, can't you see that? Or don't you care? Doesn't it mean a thing to you that my father died only last week? Haven't you any idea at all what that means?'

She felt Griff come close behind her, felt his hands on her upper arms, sensed the firm strength in them, the power in his long fingers. For a moment she wanted to lean back, let his power enfold her, rest in his strength—but that was out of the question, and she stiffened under his touch.

'Yes,' he said quietly in her ear, and her hair stirred under his breath, 'yes, Trina, of course I understand. And I wasn't making fun—just trying to lighten what seemed to be an awkward moment. It doesn't have to be awkward, you know. Just let yourself relax—forget the feelings you've obviously been harbouring about me—and let's talk like two civilised beings.'

'*I'm* civilised,' she said at once, and she could feel him smile.

'Then there's nothing to worry about. Come and sit down.'

Reluctantly she allowed him to lead her to an armchair. She would have liked nothing better than to tell him she wanted nothing to do with him, that they had nothing to talk about—but she knew that this was impossible. Her father's will had forced her into this position of not only having to talk to Griff but to work with him as well—an intolerable position, she thought, her bewilderment flooding back again. *Why* had her father done this, when he surely must have known her feelings about Griff? Hadn't he trusted her? And if not—why *Griff*? Why not Robert Nicklin or any of the other directors?

'I saw Henry Ambrose driving away as I arrived,' Griff said, sitting down opposite her. 'I presume he came to talk to you about the will.'

'Yes, that's right.' Trina had to curb her instinctive desire to tell him to mind his own business—it *was* his business.

'Did you have any idea of the provisions before this?' He spoke delicately, as if to spare her feelings, but she thought cynically that this was probably the last thing in his mind. He was more likely simply to want to make the interview as easy as possible for himself. He must be under no illusions as to her reaction to the news.

'No, I didn't. I hadn't any idea at all. I can't imagine what Dad was thinking of. It's—well, it's crazy!'

'Crazy? That's the last adjective I'd apply to your father.'

'I didn't say that *he* was crazy, I said—oh, it doesn't matter. It's done now, anyway, and there doesn't seem to be a thing I can do about it. Unless you——?' She raised her eyes with sudden hope, but he shook his head decisively.

'No, Trina. Sorry, but I've no intention of refusing the position. I think I can do well for Compson Crystal. More than that, I think *we* can do well. And that was your father's idea, wasn't it?'

'I suppose so.' Her agreement was begrudging. 'But I honestly don't see what there is for you to *do*. We shall just keep running along the same lines—we don't need new ideas or anything like that. We've got a steady market and——'

'My God!' he exclaimed. 'Every word you say makes it clearer just why your father did this! Trina, you just can't think like that these days! Don't you realise, *no* market is steady? Anything can fail and quite probably will. You have to be continually looking for new outlets, and that means being able to offer new styles, new lines, new products. Nobody can afford to stand still, can't you see that?'

'No, I can't, and I can't see why you should think you can patronise me either!' Trina came to her feet, her pale gold hair swinging. 'Compson Crystal has done very well so far without your brilliant new ideas and new lines. Just what are you proposing—that we should go in for pudding-basins and spectacles? Compson's have got a *name*—a name for a certain type of tableware, luxury items that command a high price. If we start making other things we'll lose some of our best customers. If that's what you want to do, you've got your own studio—make your pudding-basins there and leave us alone!'

Griff gave a snort of exasperation. 'I never said anything about pudding-basins! There are other ways of branching out, you know. The kind of thing I *have* been doing—glass sculpture——'

'Useless ornaments!' Trina bit out scornfully.

'I like to think they are things of beauty,' he countered. 'The Scandinavian glassmakers have had a great deal of success with them——'

'So let them! We'll stick to our lines, thank you very much.'

Griff stood up and came over to her. 'Trina, this arguing is going to get us nowhere. Your father left us in joint command—can't you accept that? Can't we work together for the good of the firm?'

'The good of the firm,' Trina sneered. 'What do you care about that? You learned all you could here and then left. It means nothing to you—the tradition of Compson Crystal, the loyalty that's built up among the men. Do you realise some of the men in that glassworks are second and third generation—their fathers and grandfathers worked for Compson? There are father and son teams there now, uncles and cousins. *They* didn't drain the factory dry, take all they could from the training they got here and then go off and set up on their own. They stuck with us and gave us back in good measure what we gave them. *They're* the ones who have the good of the firm at heart, Griff Tyzak—they and I. Not you—not some outsider who happens to have got on the right side of the owner and wormed into a position he would never otherwise have reached, a position he had absolutely no right to.'

'And you?' he asked quietly. 'Are you really fit and ready for such a position? A girl of twenty-five—just a designer, no better and no worse than a hundred others? Does an accident of birth make you more fit to run the factory than anyone else?'

Trina stared at him, frustration welling up inside her until she thought she must explode. With a tremendous effort, she controlled herself and answered in a voice that was equally quiet, even though it shook dangerously.

'I grew up here,' she said, feeling her hands clench into fists at her sides. 'The glassworks has been a part of my life ever since I was a child. I used to beg to be allowed to go in and watch the men at work. They all know me. I know them and I know their families.' She paused to try to control her uneven breathing. 'But that isn't all. I was still at school when you left Compson's. I knew then what I wanted to do and I worked hard to achieve it. I went to art college and when I came into the firm I went to the local glass college to learn more. I've been designing glass for nearly ten years—and yes, I do think I'm entitled to my position.'

'Being Managing Director is rather different from designing the odd wineglass,' Griff taunted her, and Trina bit her lip.

'It's different from making weird shapes and calling them art, too!' she retorted.

'But I *have* been running my own business,' he reminded her, and she turned away. There was no way she could win with this aggravating man! Somehow or other he would always get the last word. And she wondered what on earth it was that she had found so attractive about him all those years ago.

'Well, you're not running this one,' she said tightly. '*I'm* the Compson around here, don't forget, and I expect the final say in all policy matters. There will be no new lines. We carry on as before.'

'And see the firm go to the wall,' he commented. 'Is that what you really want—for the family name and all those men you've grown up with?'

Trina turned and stared at him. 'Go the wall? What are you talking about?'

'Trina,' he said in tones of exaggerated patience, 'there's a recession on, or hadn't you noticed? Maybe you've been so cushioned from reality in your little private world that you just hadn't realised. Firms are going bankrupt every day. Did you have some notion that Compson's are immune?'

'*Bankrupt?*' she whispered, feeling the colour drain from her face. '*Compson's* aren't going bankrupt! I told you, we've got a steady trade, we've got a reputation.'

'So have a lot of other firms, and it hasn't saved them. It's a cruel world out there, Trina, and the sooner you realise it the better.'

He looked at her then and his face changed. He stepped closer to her and his hand came up to her face, his fingers tracing a gentle path down her pale cheek.

'Don't look like that, Trina,' he said softly. 'It isn't going to happen tomorrow. It isn't going to happen at all, if I can help it. But you have to recognise the danger.'

Danger! That wasn't the only danger, Trina thought as her mind reeled and her body trembled under his touch. Every cell of her skin was responding to his fingers as they moved delicately down her neck and probed into the collar of her sweater. She closed her eyes momentarily, fighting for control, and felt him draw her nearer. Then his lips touched hers, tenderly at first then with an increasingly intimate pressure, and her whole body shook as she felt him press against her, his arms hard around her now and one hand holding her head as his mouth moved expertly over her own.

'That's better,' he murmured at last, his lips brushing

hers as he spoke. 'Now we're beginning to understand each other—and you'll find it's just as easy with the firm, Trina. There really isn't any need for any arguments, is there?'

Trina stiffened at once. Was this all he was after? Her compliance, both physically and in the business? Did he really think that a moment's weakness on her part would ensure her complicity in all his ideas for the running of Compson Crystal? Was he intent on seducing her for just that purpose?

With a quick, lithe movement she was out of his arms and behind the armchair, her hands gripping the leather back. Breathing quickly, her colour high, she glared at him as he blinked at her. She was gratified to see that he was at a loss—something that, she guessed, didn't happen very often.

'Don't come near me!' she warned as he took a step towards her. 'Don't touch me again—I'm not one of your little typists, ready for a quick kiss and a cuddle when no one else is looking. Nor am I looking for an affair—I've got too much else to think about just now, and anyway, I'm rather choosy! Just keep your distance, all right?'

Griff shrugged. 'If that's the way you want it. Me, I just like to keep the wheels oiled—and if a spot of physical pleasure is the way to do it you won't find me complaining. I never did believe in platonic friendship between a man and a woman, anyway. Put the two in close contact and something's bound to develop. I just happen to think it might as well be harmony rather than discord.'

'Well, I *do* believe in platonic friendship—not that I think there's going to be even that between us.' Trina moved away from the chair, towards the door. 'Look, if you don't mind, I'd like to continue this conversation another time. I'm feeling rather tired—the last few days have been pretty exhausting and there's still a lot to be sorted out.'

Griff stared at her for a moment, then nodded abruptly. 'All right. I'll be going now. I've got things to sort out myself—like somewhere to live up here. It's too far to commute from Herefordshire every day, especially if we get snow. We'll meet again, Trina, and have a long talk. By then, perhaps you'll have come to terms with the idea.' He came close to her as he passed to go through the door, and Trina shivered involuntarily as his sleeve brushed against her. 'I'll see myself out. You stay here. I'll be in touch.'

The door closed behind him and Trina leaned back against it, eyes closed. She still felt oddly weak, the memory of his kiss still bruising her lips, the feel of his hands still imprinted on her body. Whatever happened, she must never let him do *that* again—it was altogether too dangerous. And bewildering. She didn't even *like* him. He was arrogant, rude, overbearing and intolerably conceited. So why should his kiss, his touch, have that devastating effect on her?

She shook her head, unable to answer her questions, and moved across the room to the fireplace, where she stood looking down into the flickering flames for several moments. Presumably her father must have had some reason, some reason he considered good, for inflicting Griff Tyzack on her as joint Managing Director. In any event, she had no choice but to go along with it. But it wasn't going to be easy. She'd known that from the moment when Ambrose Henry had broken the unwelcome news. Now it was even more apparent.

Raising her eyes, she glanced across the room to the showcase which contained her father's favourite pieces of glass. There were only a few pieces in it, and pride of place was held by a tall chalice that glowed in the flickering light. Trina went over to the case, unlocked the door and lifted the chalice out.

Carefully she carried it over to the table by the tall window and set it down, examining it as if she had never seen it before. It was a cameo glass, its body so dark a blue as to be almost black, and the white enamelled decoration on it portrayed the scene of a Roman chariot race, the figures delicately carved to allow the blue of the glass beneath to show through in places as a pale glimmer.

It was one of the earliest pieces of cameo glass made after John Northwood had reproduced the broken Portland Vase for the British Museum in the nineteenth century, and it was one of the first pieces made by Compson Crystal after Joshua Compson had taken over the factory. Trina had known it ever since she was a small child; she had spent hours gazing at it, marvelling at the delicacy of the work, the intricacy of the carving of the enamel on the fragile glass, losing herself in its beauty. It was probably from the chalice that she had derived her first longings to design glass herself, and she knew that her father had gained an equal pleasure from gazing at it, touching it and expressing his appreciation of the artistry and genius that had gone into its making.

The Compson Chalice had been handed down through three generations, and now it had come to her. It represented all that she felt most deeply about the glass works and about her responsibilities to the factory and the men who worked there. Now an outsider had come into the firm and she could not envisage what would happen next. She stared at the chalice as though it were a crystal ball and could show her the future.

But all she could see was its beauty. And she resolved that, whatever Griff Tyzak might do or say, she would never break faith with that beauty—the beauty that, to her, symbolised the essence of Compson Crystal. They would *not* 'branch out' and try new lines and products; they would continue, as they had for three generations, to produce beautiful and useful tableware, tableware that kings and queens would be proud to use, bowls and plates and glasses that would enhance any setting and call forth admiration wherever it was seen.

As carefully as she had removed it, Trina returned the chalice to the showcase and locked the door. Then, her head high, she left the library and went into the small office her father had used at home. As she had told Griff, she had a lot to do—and the sooner she got started, the better. There was no way she was going to let Griff Tyzak get ahead of her—no way at all!

CHAPTER TWO

THE moment when she entered the glasshouse had never failed to excite Trina. She could recall the trembling anticipation she had known as a child, when her father had allowed her to come in—strictly supervised, of course—to watch the men at work. It was just as exciting whether they were making the ordinary range of wineglasses and decanters, or something really special—though at those times her father would be there too, with the other directors, watching as some beautiful new shape emerged from the glowing lump on the end of the blowing-iron. She could still remember many of these pieces—the punchbowl made for the Queen's Silver Wedding, for instance, and the rose-bowl for the Jubilee. More recently, there had been the elegant table set for the Prince of Wales' wedding, which she herself had helped design.

On those occasions the directors had all attended to watch the first piece made, and excitement had rippled like a wave through the whole factory. But Trina loved it just as much when she wandered through alone, talking to the men she had known all her life, getting to know newer arrivals, and watching the process that never failed to fascinate her, the transformation of molten glass into something useful and lovely.

Today was her first visit since her father's funeral. She felt slightly nervous, her emotions rather near the surface. So many things had changed; she was no longer the Managing Director's daughter, with her own position within the factory; she was Managing Director herself—or joint, she reminded herself bitterly—and although the men had always been her friends she wasn't entirely sure how they would take to what they would no doubt term 'petticoat government'. Nor had she any idea how they would react to Griff. Many of

26

them knew him, had worked with him, even taught him. What would they think of his sudden return and promotion?

She went through the furnace-room, smiling a greeting at the teasers who tended the great furnace, ensuring that it never went out so that the huge dome above was always at the high temperature to melt the mixture of sand, red lead and broken glass to make the 'metal' used by the blowers in the glasshouse. The steps up to the glasshouse were bare and stark, but as she opened the door at the top she was struck, as always, by the vibrant life and colour within.

At this time of year, the warmth was welcome; it was less so in summer when the men would strip to the waist, muscles gleaming in the red glow of the furnace. Even now they were mostly wearing little more than light T-shirts and the sweat ran off them as they worked. No wonder they needed their bottles of cold tea, which stood everywhere around the cavernous foundry. There were no signs of food; eating in the glasshouse was forbidden because of the danger from the red lead used in mixing the batch. At 'baggin-time' the men would go to eat their breakfast outside, returning to work as soon as possible. Nobody shirked much on piece-time.

Trina stood by the door, watching quietly and unnoticed. She had always felt that the glasshouse had a faintly Dickensian air about it, with its domed furnace in the centre surrounded by the glowing mouths of the pots, filled with the molten glass that was gathered on the blowing-irons in red-gold lumps, like fiery toffee-apples, to be taken to the footmaker, the servitor or the gaffer who rolled and blew it into shape. The scene was of constant, unhurried movement; the men looked almost casual as they moved to and fro and she admired again, as she always had, the way the footmaker allowed exactly the right amount of metal to accumulate on the end and swinging it rhythmically to allow the gob to cool and lengthen. Then he would settle himself in his chair—a crude bench with sturdy arms on which he could roll the metal before plunging it into the steam-mould to shape it, blowing down the long iron and snatching his thumb on to the end before air could escape. It was all done so swiftly, yet without apparent urgency, that almost before Trina knew it another wineglass had been made before her eyes and the iron thrown like a long spear to the bit-gatherer, who caught it at the last second before the still glowing end touched the floor, and returned it to the hot shoe beside the pot, for reheating.

One of the men in the chair nearest her glanced up and caught her eye. Trina smiled at him and moved closer.

'Hullo, Steve. How's it going?'

'Not so bad, Miss Trina. We're getting along nice with this lot.' He hesitated. 'All the lads are pleased you're taking over, miss. We'll miss your old dad, though.'

'Yes, so will I.' She wondered if they knew yet about Griff. Probably it would be best to call the men together in the canteen and tell them exactly what was going to happen. That would be easy, if she knew herself, she thought wryly. But she hadn't seen Griff since his visit to Compson House; presumably he was busy getting his studio sorted out and finding somewhere nearby to live.

Steve had begun to marver another lump of metal and she moved on, nodding and smiling at the other men in their 'chairs'—teams of four or five so accustomed to each other's movements and timing that they moved with the nonchalant precision of a modern ballet. Every few seconds a young apprentice would take a newly-made piece of glass to the big grey *lehr* that stood in the middle of the glasshouse—the long cooling oven through which the glass travelled slowly to the process shop, where the tops of glasses would be cracked off and the rims melted to smooth the edge. Production was constant and high, and although it looked so easy, Trina was well aware of the skill and sheer hard work that was involved in glass-making.

Like her father, she believed in letting the men know of her appreciation.

Moving round the glasshouse, she came to the casterole chair where larger items were made—bowls, decanters, jugs and so on. The 'gaffer' here was Trevor Hodgetts, one of the most expert workers in the factory; swarthy and sometimes uncommunicative, he had taken over the chair from his father, and his own nephew worked in the factory as well; his younger son was due to start in the summer. Trina stopped for a few moments to watch him at work and remembered that, although he was a few years older than Griff, the two of them had been apprentices together. What would he think, she wondered, of his old workmate's new position?

'Morning, Miss Trina,' Trevor said, raising his voice easily above the clatter that was continually going on around them. 'We're getting on with those jugs you designed—that new shape, see? Seems to be coming out all right.'

'Oh, yes, it does.' Trina looked appreciatively at the new jugs, watching as Trevor made the next one as casually as if he had done nothing else all his life. The shape formed as she watched, changing from an amorphous lump to a graceful, curved vessel that would be used in a thousand homes. Not so many of these were made each day, of course; the large size involved at least one reheating in a small furnace, or glory-hole, during its creation, and although Trevor appeared nonchalant enough, Trina knew that he was in fact bringing all his concentration and skill to bear as he worked.

As he handed the jug over to be taken to the handle-maker, he turned back to Trina, his brows drawn together in a heavy frown that, she knew, denoted deep feeling rather than anger.

'That was a good funeral your dad had,' he announced abruptly. 'Fitting. Most of us went, you know.'

'Yes, I know,' Trina said gently. She had been much

touched by the sight of the men, all in their best suits, filling the church where so many glassmakers had been buried. Their voices, raised in hymn instead of the more secular songs they often sang in the foundry, had almost lifted the roof at times; afterwards, they had filed quietly outside and stood at a respectful distance while the family and immediate friends followed the coffin to the graveside. Nothing had been said; none of them had approached Trina directly; but she had been overwhelmingly conscious of their sympathy and their own sorrow at the death of the man they had known for so long. It was all an integral part of the close loyalty that had developed in the works, the family atmosphere that was very precious to Trina and an important part of her determination to resist change.

'How are your family, Trevor?' she asked, and his face twisted wryly.

'All right, I suppose. Daughter wants to get married in the spring. Eighteen, I ask you! Seen nothing, done nothing, and can't think of anything better than to tie herself down the minute she's out of school. Not like you, Miss Trina. Got a bit of sense, you have.'

'What does your wife think about it?' Trina asked, hiding a smile. She knew quite well that Trevor had married at only twenty-one and was fairly sure that his wife had probably been two or three years younger.

'Oh, the Bride's all for it,' he answered, using his accustomed term for the dumpy little woman he still thought the world of. 'Well, why not—*she* did all right, didn't she? Married me! But our Carol—well, I dunno. Still, nothing you can do about it these days, is there?' He turned away to take the next iron and begin his fashioning all over again. 'Be glad of all the work I can get, though, to pay for the wedding!'

Trina watched him for a few minutes and then crossed the floor to where Alf Bridgens was making handles for the jugs. Alf was the oldest man in the factory. He had been there when her grandfather, son of old Joshua, had been in charge, and his tales of old times had kept her enthralled on many occasions. He told her of the days when the glassmakers of the whole area had held parades through the streets, exhibiting the glass swords, trumpets and yards of ale that had been made in their spare time. Known as friggers, these items were still made, often during the lunch-breaks or by apprentices learning new skills. Trina herself had been given a variety of glass ornaments and novelties— swans, fruits, a 'flip-flop', which had once been a common toy among glassmakers' children, and a glass elephant that she still treasured. Griff had given it to her when she was just ten, she recalled now, and that had probably marked the beginning of her childish adoration of him. Not that she kept the elephant for any sentimental reason, she quickly assured herself; simply because it was attractive and funny and she liked it.

She continued her tour through the process-shop, to the cutting shop where the glass was decorated. Here the beauty of shape was enhanced by the decoration; the copper-wheel engraving, done freehand, and the precision of the straight cutting and the intaglio which could be combined to make an infinite variety of patterns, from the geometric designs of diamond shapes and criss-cross lines to the flowing, scooped-out representation of leaves and flowers.

It was here that Trina's own work was done, and she paused to speak to many of the cutters and the intaglio workers. Most of the designs were ones she had worked on, and she never lost the thrill of seeing her own ideas actually taking shape in glass. She stayed for a long time, watching a new wineglass design being perfected, and talking to the men who were executing it. Then she went across to the two engravers—artists in their own right, making pictures on glass, either from their own imagination and observation, or to some specified requirement; or simply engraving names or initials for some special event, perhaps an eighteenth birthday or a silver wedding anniversary.

'Hullo, Derek,' said Trina, stopping beside them. 'I've been wondering where you'd got to.'

Derek Paton glanced up and smiled. He was a little older than Trina, and they had known each other all their lives, attended the same school and, when Trina left art college and came into the factory, had gone on day-release together to learn more about glass. Derek was quiet and self-effacing; highly talented, he rarely pushed himself forward but preferred to get on with his work, keeping apart from disputes. Trina was very fond of him and it had occurred to her once or twice that he would make a very good husband.

'You had a lot on your plate,' he said now, his hazel eyes serious. 'I couldn't intrude—but if there's anything I can do now. . . .'

Yes, there is, there is, Trina wanted to cry. You can tell me how to cope with Griff Tyzak's eruption into my life—*he* doesn't have any scruples about intruding! You can tell me why my father made that condition, why he forced me to share responsibility for the firm with *him*, of all people. You can make me feel safe, secure, confident. . . .

She couldn't say any of this aloud, but Derek seemed to know that she needed support. He laid his hand over hers where it rested on his bench and said quietly: 'Perhaps you need a change of scene, Trina. Would you like to come out for a meal one evening? You must be lonely, all by yourself in that big house.'

Trina felt a wash of gratitude. An evening out—it seemed a lifetime since she'd done that, and in a way it was, for she hadn't been out socially since her father's death. And a few hours in Derek's undemanding company could be just what she needed, restoring her sense of proportion, even helping her to get Griff Tyzak's dynamic impact into some kind of proportion. With Derek behind her, believing in her, she would be more able to stand up to him—and, at the same time, control the quick, fiery temper that she suspected could land her in trouble if she lost it with Griff.

'That would be lovely,' she said gratefully. 'Could we make it tonight? I really feel I need to get out again.'

'Sure. What about the Swan, at Bridgnorth? They

usually do a good meal there, and it's quiet and comfortable.'

'That'll be fine.' Trina's eyes misted. She hadn't quite realised until now how much she longed for someone to care, to cherish her. Her father had done so ever since she could remember—all the more so, perhaps, after his wife had died—and in the days since his own death she had missed him badly, feeling the loss of his strength and support just when she needed them most.

'I'll come out to Compson House and pick you up. About seven?' Derek bent his head back to his work, and Trina smiled and left him, moving on with a feeling of being warmed and comforted. She knew that the evening ahead would be pleasant and happy, just like all the evenings she had spent with Derek; there was never any tension between them. Not like the tension, the almost electric vibrations that pulsed the air between her and Griff, bringing all her nerves alive and sending a sharp tingling awareness coursing through her veins. . . .

Reaching her own office at last, Trina sifted quickly through the mail. There was much more of it now, and a good deal of it she would need advice on—better get Robert Nicklin or one of the other directors along to give her a hand. She was faintly surprised at the amount and variety of mail the Managing Director received. Another of those things she had taken for granted while her father was alive.

Sitting at her desk, she let her mind stray back to the days when her father was alive and well, fully in charge. She had been so close to him; closer than many daughters to their fathers, perhaps, because her mother had died years ago, when Trina was only three years old. It had been a tragic accident—she had drowned while on holiday in Cornwall—but William Compson, shattered though he must have been, had been determined that the loss would have no more effect than was absolutely unavoidable on the child who had lost her mother. From that day on he had been both parents to Trina, sublimating his grief in caring for her, so that she had grown up hardly missing the parent she had lost. Instead, father and daughter had grown close, and if life had appeared to be easy for Trina after that it was because what she wanted for herself her father had wanted for her, and because she knew him so well that she instinctively pleased him.

Life was going to seem very empty from now on, she thought, realising the depth of her loss more sharply than at any time since William's death. There had been so much to do and think about that she had barely had time for grieving; now the tears came almost before she was aware of them, pouring like rain from her eyes and soaking the letters that lay before her on the desk.

The door swung open before she had time to recover herself and a deep voice exclaimed: 'Oh, there you are, Trina—I've been looking everywhere for you. Nicklin said you were somewhere in the factory—what's the matter? You're crying!'

Oh God, no! As if things weren't bad enough already—but *he* had to find her crying! Trina rubbed her hand hastily across her face and wiped the letters with her sleeve. She looked up, only too aware of the tear-stains still on her cheeks, and met Griff's gaze with more than a touch of defiance that stemmed as much from her own nerve-tingling awareness of him as from hostility.

'What is it, Trina?' he asked before she could speak, and she felt another quick surge of grief at his question.

'What do you think?' she asked, her voice trembling. 'It's my first day back—my first day here without Dad—aren't I entitled to feel something? Isn't it natural, for goodness' sake?'

'Well, yes, of course it is——'

'Well then!' she snapped. 'And there's no need to look at me as if I were made of glass myself—I'm quite all right. It was just—just for a minute——' Her voice trembled again but she pulled herself together with determination. 'What did you want, anyway? I thought you were back in Herefordshire.'

'Only to get things tidied up.' He came further into

the office and closed the door. 'I rather thought we could go through the mail together—see what needs doing, get some kind of policy formulated——'

'I told you before, the policy stands. There's no need to change anything.'

'And *I* told *you* that that was a matter of opinion.'

'Your opinion, perhaps,' she said quickly. 'I don't happen to share it, and I doubt if any of the other directors will.'

'You've been talking to them, then?'

'No, of course not, I——'

'Well, I have. And I think you'll find that more than one supports me. The firm needs some new life injected into it. Oh, it's coasting along quite nicely, I agree—but that isn't good enough these days. Things can happen very quickly and once the rot sets in it tends to gallop.'

'There's no rot in Compson Crystal——' Trina began angrily, but Griff lifted one eyebrow cynically.

'No? Well, you may be right—but there's no harm in prevention, is there? Nor in setting up new lines, extending our reputation in case the traditional ones fall out of favour——'

'Oh, you're not still on that, are you?' Trina turned away, as if to indicate that the subject wasn't worth her time in discussing. 'I told you, there's more risk in doing that than in keeping things as they are. A new line takes time to find a market—it's bound to represent a loss to begin with. And that's just what we *can't* risk at the present time. We're better off to keep going as we are.'

'So you admit that the firm isn't as stable as it could be,' he remarked coolly, and Trina snorted with exasperation.

'I'm not admitting anything of the kind! *Nobody's* in a state to take risks at present. Look, I can't waste time arguing this morning—there's a lot to be done. Why don't you go and—and—— ' She stopped, unable to think of anything to suggest he could do. Oh, why had he come here at all? Why *ever* had her father made that condition? She bit her lip in frustration and Griff, watching her enigmatically, smiled.

'You seem to have forgotten that my job is to share just those tasks which are making you so busy,' he pointed out maddeningly. 'Joint M.D., remember? Why don't we sit down and go through these letters together?' He pulled a chair up to the desk and drew a pile of envelopes towards him. 'I'll go through these, shall I, and pick out the ones I think need further discussion. Will that be all right?'

Trina found her voice. 'No, it will *not* be all right! I want to see *all* the letters—I need to know all that's going on. *I'll* look through them first, and *if* there's anything I think you can help me with——' her tone made it clear that she thought this highly unlikely '—well, I'll ask you.'

'Oh, no,' he said silkily. 'I think we both need to know it all, don't you? At least for the time being. But we don't have to be childish about it. I'll tell you what we'll do. We'll each have a pile, make notes, swap and then compare. How does that suit you?'

'It strikes me as a waste of valuable time,' Trina said between her teeth, and Griff nodded.

'I'm inclined to agree with you there, at least. But until we can trust each other I can see no other way, can you? And you don't trust me, do you? Not an inch. Though I'm not quite sure what you expect me to do— sabotage the whole future of the firm in some way, is that it?'

'You don't trust me either,' Trina retorted, and he smiled.

'No, I don't. But I think I've got good reason to distrust you, Trina. You've made it more than clear that you don't welcome me here, that you neither understand nor agree with your father's wishes, and that nothing would give you greater pleasure than to see me leave Stourbridge and go back to Herefordshire, never to darken your doorstep again. I wouldn't put it past you to find some way of making sure that happens, if only it were possible. So I'd be a fool to trust you, wouldn't I?' His dark eyes held her gaze for a moment until she looked away, then with a smile in his voice he said: 'So let's not waste any more of our valuable time, hmm? Let's make a start on this mail.'

Trina felt helpless. Some way or another, Griff would always win. She watched as his strong fingers sorted through the envelopes, lifting out the ones that looked most interesting, leaving others until later. He worked quickly, reading and making notes, placing the letters in neat piles. There was no hint in his behaviour that he was new to the factory; he seemed quite competent, well able to take over and run things entirely to his own satisfaction.

So what am I doing here? Trina wondered dully. I might as well go back to designing—at least there I can be sure I'm doing something worthwhile.

As she watched, she couldn't help noticing the strength and power of his hands; the long, tapering fingers, the muscular wrists. She felt her own pulses quicken and suppressed an irrational longing to lay her own fingers on those wrists, to feel the warmth of his skin under her own.

Quickly she pulled a pile of letters towards her and began opening them at random, hardly taking in the contents. Her heart was thumping and she scolded herself bitterly. What was she thinking of—Griff Tyzak was nothing to her, nothing! All right, he had a certain presence, a glamour even with his black hair and velvet-brown eyes, his powerful body and the height which made him look almost slender despite his breadth. He had that devastating smile too, that she remembered from the days of her teenage adulation; he didn't seem to want to use it on her now. And maybe that was just as well! The way she was feeling now, it wouldn't take much for her to forget all her principles and let him have his own way in anything he wanted.

And that was just what mustn't happen! This unexpected and unwanted effect that Griff had on her was just about the most dangerous thing about him. If she didn't keep her responses under control, if ever he became aware of them, there would be no holding him. He would do just what he liked in the firm, making changes, experimenting, ruining everything her father and grandfather had worked for, risking the livelihoods of all those men out there, who depended on Compson Crystal. He would take over completely and there wouldn't be a thing she could do to stop him.

And all that was quite apart from anything he might do to her.

Trina shivered suddenly. It was just a physical thing, she told herself, nothing more. Perhaps it was some kind of reaction from the shock of her father's death. She mustn't give way to it; mustn't let it affect her determination to keep faith with the tradition of family and firm. It meant nothing—nothing at all.

Griff glanced up suddenly and caught her eye. To her dismay, she felt a blush stain her cheeks and saw him looking at her thoughtfully before he spoke.

'You're looking tired,' he said. 'Why don't you go along home? I can deal with most of this.'

Tears pricked Trina's eyes and she brushed them away quickly. He wasn't going to fool her that way! 'No, thank you,' she said coldly. 'I'm quite all right and I'd rather stay.'

He shrugged. 'As you like. Well, there doesn't seem to be anything here that's going to cause any trouble. Now, about letting the men know the position——'

'I thought we ought to have a meeting,' Trina said quickly. 'Call them all into the canteen, perhaps, and tell them just what's happening. They'll be relieved to know nothing's going to change.'

'If indeed that is the case.' Griff watched her as if expecting an outburst at this, but Trina said nothing. 'Before we do that, then, we should have a board meeting and decide just what the position is. Shall we arrange that for tomorrow morning?'

Trina began to feel that she was being steamrollered. But on the other hand, wouldn't it be a good idea—to show him that the other directors were with her in this matter? That would put a stop to his ideas of branching out, whatever they might be. Joint Managing Director he might be, but he wouldn't be able to push his ideas through if she and everyone else were against them. And she was quite confident that the other directors—Robert Nicklin, who had come up from the factory floor, becoming first Works Manager and then Works Director, John Ballard, Graham Gordon and the others—would back her in this. They had all known and worked with her father; none of them would want radical change the moment he was gone.

'There's one other thing,' Griff went on, frowning over a letter he was holding in his hand. 'This approach from an Arab oil state—you never mentioned that to me.'

'I never saw any need to. Is that letter from the Embassy? May I see it, please?' Trina reached across, her fingers trembling with anger as he held it just too far away for her to grasp. 'Griff, please! That letter is my business—I've been dealing with it all along.'

'A possible order for two thousand pieces, as part of the celebrations for a family wedding,' Griff read, his black brows drawn together in a frown. 'You saw no need to tell me about this? Didn't it occur to you that this is a very large order indeed and could mean a great deal to Compson Crystal?'

'Of course it occurred to me!' Trina snapped. 'I know very well what it means. But it isn't certain yet, Griff—we've had to submit designs for it and I know we're in competition with several other glassworks—there's no point in counting on it. We just have to wait and see.'

'*Wait and see?* Trina, that's no way to get business! You have to keep on at them—don't let them forget we exist, keep showing them new things. What have they seen so far? What new designs have you shown them? Just what do they want—this is *important*, Trina, don't you realise?'

'Of *course* I realise! What do you take me for? And what do you think my father was doing until the day he died? We put everything we knew into the designs we submitted—we all worked on them. And I just happen to think we did quite well. But having done that, there's nothing else we *can* do. We just have to wait and hope for the best.'

Griff half rose and leaned over the desk, thumping it with his clenched fist. 'Wait and hope for the best? Like children waiting for Santa to call? Trina, I can hardly believe that you're actually *saying* these things! Waiting and hoping are just what you *don't* have to do. There must be things you haven't thought of, designs you haven't considered. Coloured glass, for instance—did you include any of that? Glasses with gold rims—were they among your designs? Or was it all plain crystal, the same old stuff that you've done over and over again?'

'It was seeing that same old stuff that made them come to us in the first place,' Trina retorted. 'As for gold-rimmed glass, yes, we did include some designs for that. But *coloured* glass—no! We don't use colour, Griff, or maybe you hadn't noticed. We didn't submit any coloured designs at all. It's not our style.'

'Not our *style*?' For a moment, she thought he would explode. His eyes burned like deep flames in his dark face. 'Trina, haven't you got it into your head yet that our *style* has to be what the customer wants—not what *we* decide he should have! We have to show him anything and everything we could possibly produce—if we don't do that, how is he to know our capabilities? How will you feel if he looks at our designs and then goes off and orders a whole range of coloured glass from a competitor? Something that he might well have ordered from us if only we'd let him know we were willing to produce it.'

'But we're *not* willing! Compson's have made their name on clear lead crystal. That's what people want, what they come to us for——'

'And wouldn't they come to us for coloured glass if we only started to make it? Couldn't we make a name for that too?'

Trina stared at him, then dropped her head on to her hand in despair. Were they to spend the rest of their lives arguing this point? She sought for more words, but before she could speak Griff was talking again, his voice quick and eager, pressing his point home.

'The Arabs *like* coloured glass, Trina. They like colour and richness and flamboyance. Did you take that into account when you made your designs? Did you consider their tastes at all? Or did you just give them a variation on a theme—the theme you've been playing for the past ten years or more?'

'Well, of *course* we considered their tastes. We did a lot of research on it—looked at designs that had gone down well previously in those countries—the table settings that were made for Baghdad and Jedda, for instance; we were able to get samples of the designs used by the company that made those. And we showed them samples of what we were making now and asked which they liked best. The Sheikh himself came up here when he was on a visit to England and we showed him all kinds of things. He wanted a design that would be unique to his glass, of course, and we used the falcon that's part of his family crest in the final submission.'

'Hm.' Griff seemed reluctant to be impressed by this catalogue, and Trina suppressed her anger. Just who did he think he was anyway? Her father had been in on all the discussions that had been held about the Arabian order and he had been quite satisfied with the designs she had produced. Just who was Griff Tyzak to start throwing his weight about?

'But you never thought to suggest coloured glass?' he persisted, and Trina sighed with exasperation.

'No, we didn't. He never even mentioned it himself. Griff, have you any idea what it would mean to turn over to colours now? It means new materials—gold chloride, tin oxide, all that kind of thing. It means much slower cooling—the *lehr* would have to be adjusted to suit that glass and would slow down production of all the rest. It means several pots having to be kept for just that colour. And it means trial and error to get the colour right. We just aren't set up for it, surely you can see that?'

'None of those problems are insuperable, and it could mean opening up a whole new market——'

'Which we don't need. We *have* our market, Griff, and we're satisfied with it. We don't need to take risks such as you're suggesting.'

They were both on their feet now, facing each other across the desk. Trina's eyes flashed green with anger and she pushed back her pale hair with a shaking hand. Was there no way to convince this stubborn man? Was he determined to risk the future of Compson Crystal for a whim? And why was he so set on change anyway? Why was he so determined to introduce such radical alterations?

Griff's lean face was livid with suppressed rage, and he was breathing fast. At any moment Trina felt that he might reach across and shake her by the shoulders; suddenly frighteningly aware of his strength and her own vulnerability, she backed away from him, her eyes on the harsh lines of his face. Hadn't her father realised it would be like this? Hadn't he known that she and Griff would never agree—that whatever the issue, his betrayal of ten years ago would invariably come between them, making it impossible for them to take each other seriously?

Not that it seemed to worry Griff. He seemed to think that what he had done had been perfectly justified. But to Trina, it was a defection amounting almost to treason, and she could never forget it.

'Let's just get one thing clear, Trina,' Griff said at last. He spoke slowly and clearly, as if addressing a small child. 'You seem to think that coloured glass is something new, something revolutionary. You don't seem to have studied the history of your own company. Don't you realise that coloured glass was among the earliest glass produced by Compson Crystal—that the firm *began* by making it? That it had a pretty good reputation for colours before it ever went into lead crystal and cut-glass in a big way? I'm not suggesting any new departures, Trina—I'm simply advocating a revival. Is that so very terrible? Is it so very *un*traditional?'

Trina gazed at him. She could find no words to

answer him. What he said was quite true and she knew it—and she knew too that she had completely forgotten the origins of the firm and its early products.

'I don't want to turn the whole factory over to colours,' he went on persuasively. 'Just start again in a small way—see what the reaction is among the retailers and customers. And this Arabian order could be an ideal opportunity to make a start, don't you agree?' He moved closer and lifted his hand to push back a strand of fair hair. 'Like the ad says, Trina, you know it makes sense. Doesn't it? Isn't it just your feminine pride that's stopping you from saying yes?'

Trina stared up at him. You could drown in those lake-brown eyes, she thought dizzily. But there was no warmth in them—only a cold sensuality. Griff Tyzak was clearly as expert in manipulating women as he was in manipulating glass. And as he came closer still, so that the tips of her breasts brushed against his broad chest and a tingle of excitement ran through her whole body, Trina knew that he wouldn't stop at any way of manipulating her—mentally or physically. Griff Tyzak's sensuality would be used to getting just exactly what he wanted, in more ways than one.

Well, it might have worked for him up to now, but it wasn't going to work any more. No man had succeeded yet in making Trina Compson do anything she didn't want to do, and she wasn't about to change now. He might be right about coloured glass and he might be wrong—but this wasn't going to be the way he persuaded her.

Her heart thumping uncomfortably against her ribs, she moved sideways away from him. The letter from the Embassy lay open on the desk and she stretched out a hand and tweaked it away before he could stop her. Then, with a quick twist of her body, she was at the door, flushed and triumphant.

'You can leave this with me, Griff,' she told him, flourishing the letter. 'I'll see to it. Though there isn't really much to do at this stage—as you've seen, it's only a tentative proposal, to see if we could meet their requirements in the time available. There's nothing firm about it yet.'

Griff turned slowly. The expression on his face was unreadable, but Trina would have taken bets that he was flaming with anger inside. A round to me, she thought gloatingly—then shivered as she met his eyes, as hard and cold as stone, and knew that he wouldn't be content to let things rest there. She might have won a round, but there were still a good many more to come.

'All right,' he said quietly, and the menace in his voice sent a shudder through Trina's heart. 'All right. You take your letter. But I'll see the next one that comes, Trina. Just as I'll see everything else that comes into this office. You'll not forget that we're *joint* Managing Directors, with joint responsibilities. That's the way your father wanted it and it's the way the shareholders want it. Any attempt on your part to keep the business of the firm from me will get you into very deep trouble.'

Trina stared at him. 'Are—are you threatening me?' she asked, her voice shaking, and he shrugged.

'If that's the way you want to look at it, yes. But all I'm really doing is reminding you of the correct procedure.' He was beside her now and his long fingers reached out and lifted her chin, turning her face so that she was forced to meet his eyes. 'Don't forget it, Trina. I wouldn't like to see you lose that position you value so highly.'

He shouldered his way past her and out of the office. And Trina stood there, trembling uncontrollably, her fingers moving slowly over her lips.

For some reason, they felt bruised. As if she had been brutally and mercilessly kissed.

CHAPTER THREE

THE Swan was a pleasant hotel in the middle of Bridgnorth; outside, it was of an attractive black and white beamed construction, inside the pattern was followed with oak beams and a low balustrade separating the dining area from the pub lounge. Red carpet gave a warm, welcoming atmosphere, and Trina felt herself begin to relax slightly for the first time that day—or at any time since Ambrose Henry had first broken the news of her father's will.

Derek had booked a table, but the hotel wasn't crowded when they arrived and they sat for a while in deep armchairs, not talking much. There wasn't much, Trina discovered, that she could say—or was it that there was too much, and once she began she wouldn't know how or when to stop?

She leaned back and closed her eyes. In an effort to shake off the peculiar apprehension that seemed to be permanently tightening her stomach lately, she had changed her daytime gear of jeans and sweater for a brighter outfit; she now wore a thick, soft knitted jacket in a medley of brilliant hues, over an equally colourful sweater and slinky black trousers that fitted the curves of her slender figure like a second skin. Over the jacket, knotted loosely around her neck, she wore a lacy yellow shawl, and as she grew warmer she shrugged the jacket off and let it rest loosely on her shoulders.

Derek had seemed faintly shocked when he had called for her at Compson House, immaculate in his dark suit and plain shirt and tie. Probably thought she was being disrespectful to her father's memory, she thought wryly. But Dad wouldn't have wanted her to go about looking dowdy—he'd always been proud of her looks, encouraging her to make the most of them even when it had meant wearing the rather way-out styles she had gone in for while she was at art college. And he had known that the way she looked had quite an effect on her confidence. He would have understood that, even if she wasn't about to meet Griff Tyzak, she needed to build herself up in preparation for the next time.

At least, she had always thought he would have understood her, whatever she did. Now, with the will and its impositions never far from her thoughts, she was beginning to wonder about that. Just what *had* his reasons been? Did Griff know? Did *anyone* know?

'How are you feeling about things now?' Derek enquired, breaking into her thoughts. 'Must be pretty strange for you—taking over so suddenly. There wasn't any hint, was there? I mean, your father wasn't ill beforehand, was he?'

Trina shook her head. 'No, not at all. He just—well, he just seemed to fall asleep after lunch that day and—and that was that. No pain, or anything. Just—finish.'

'Mm. The way everyone says they wish they could go.' Derek looked at her with understanding. 'A shock for you, though.'

'Yes, it was. I just didn't realise what had happened. When I did—well, it was too late.' She bit her lip. 'It would have been too late anyway, Dr Mansfield said. And I couldn't be sorry for Dad. He hated the idea of growing old and helpless. It's just that—well, life seems rather empty without him.'

'You were pretty close, weren't you?'

'Yes. I suppose we were bound to be, with my mother dying so young. I don't remember her at all, you know. Dad's always been the main figure in my life.' She heard her voice tremble and took a sip of her drink. 'Nannies and so on—I had those, he had to do that because of the factory—but it was always Dad at the centre of it all. And he made sure he had plenty of spare time to spend with me.'

'It must have helped that you were interested in the factory,' Derek said thoughtfully, and Trina nodded.

'Oh yes. I loved it right from the start. I'd have been

there every day if I could—and when I got old enough to have holiday jobs I just lived for them! Didn't mind what I did—until the design office became my chief interest. I did my first design when I was fourteen! It wasn't produced commercially, but Dad had a set of wineglasses made for himself and I've still got them at home.'

She finished her drink and sat for a few moments staring into space. That close partnership was over now, and she was only just beginning to realise fully what it had meant to her. The encouragement, the quiet confidence that her father had always shown in her— these had boosted her morale, helped her through the times when she had wondered if she would ever make it as a designer. They had helped her right up to the day he had died—and then had been abruptly withdrawn. She didn't know yet just how much she had depended on them—how capable she was of managing without such support. And before she had had time to find out, Griff Tyzak had burst into her life, without any respect at all for her abilities, determined—it seemed—to put her down at every opportunity.

But did she really have to manage on her own? Trina looked across at Derek, noting his pleasantly good-humoured face, his friendly hazel eyes, the tolerant lines of his mouth. Couldn't she find, with Derek, the comfort and security that she craved? Wasn't he, after all, just the opposite from the abrasive Griff—warm, easygoing, ready to listen to her, acknowledge her ability? They'd known each other all their lives; wasn't that a good basis for understanding?

Derek seemed to sense her feelings. He didn't say any more about her father but got up and led her over to their table. Trina slipped into the seat against the wall, from where she could see over the balustrade across the lounge. There were a few more people in now and a pleasant hum of conversation was beginning to fill the air.

Together, they studied the menu. Rather to her surprise, Trina found that she was hungry, and realised that she hadn't eaten a really substantial meal since her father's death, in spite of Mrs Aston's efforts. Perhaps that accounted for her nerviness, she thought, and determined to make up for it now. She chose a thick vegetable soup followed by roast beef and Yorkshire pudding.

'Good home cooking,' Derek commented. 'I'll have the same—don't think you can do better. But you usually go for something more adventurous, Trina—doesn't sole Meunière or chicken Kiev appeal tonight?'

She shook her head. 'Not really. I think I'm thumb-sucking—going back to the homely things for comfort. Back to the days when everything was safe and cosy.'

Derek looked faintly puzzled. 'But everything's all right now, isn't it?' he queried. 'I mean—well, that was tactless, I know, in the circumstances. But your position's assured, isn't it—you've stepped into your father's shoes. And you've got Griff Tyzak coming in to help you. You haven't really got anything to worry about.'

Trina gazed at him. How little he knew! Could he really mean it? Could he *really* believe that the changeover could be so smooth? That her position was unassailable—and that Griff would be not only helpful but welcome?

But Derek was quite plainly not joking, nor was he being cynical. He smiled at her, obviously really believing what he'd said. Trina opened her mouth to put him right—and then closed it again.

If Derek hadn't been able to see the truth for himself, she doubted if she could explain it to him.

Their soup arrived and Trina took a mouthful. Perhaps she was being unreasonable—after all, how was Derek to know her feelings about Griff? As far as she remembered, they had never really discussed him. She thought back over the years she and Derek had been friends. Almost always, really. Had she told him how she felt about Griff—and about his leaving the factory? She doubted if Derek had known about the teenage crush she had had for the older man—but she surely hadn't made any secret of her sense of betrayal when Griff had left.

'How do *you* feel about Griff Tyzak?' she asked, and found herself unexpectedly anxious about his reply.

'Well, of course, it's years since I saw him.' Derek broke his bread roll. 'But we always got on very well together. Not that I saw an awful lot of him, but he seemed a good chap to have around. Very highly talented, of course.'

'I didn't really mean that,' Trina said unreasonably. 'I mean, how do you feel about him coming into the factory again—at this stage? After leaving us in the lurch like he did.'

'Did he leave you in the lurch?' Derek seemed genuinely suprised. 'I didn't realise that, Trina.'

'Well, of *course* he did,' Trina said impatiently. 'We'd trained him, hadn't we—Dad gave him the chance of an apprenticeship without knowing a thing about him—he didn't even come from this area. His mother lived in Wales and his father had some incurable disease, hadn't worked for years. He had no glass background at all.'

'Hadn't he? But Tyzak's a name that's always been connected with glass, surely? Isn't it one of the old Huguenot names?'

Trina dismissed this with a wave of her hand. 'That doesn't mean a thing. People scatter, they don't all follow in father's footsteps. Perhaps way back there was some connection—but it had obviously been dead for years.'

'Still, there must have been something,' Derek argued. 'When you think of his talent. I've watched him at work. He could do anything with glass. He could practically make it sit up and beg. I'm sure that must have been inherited.'

Trina sighed and laid down her spoon. This conversation wasn't going the way she wanted it at all. The waiter arrived and took away their soup plates, and she waited until the main course had been served before speaking again.

'All right,' she resumed, leaning forward. 'So Griff's

a talented man. Don't you think it was a betrayal to take that talent away from the factory that helped him to develop it? Don't you think he should have stayed with us, given *us* the benefit of his skills instead of setting up in opposition——'

'Oh, hardly in opposition,' Derek objected. 'I mean, he's not making the same kind of thing at all. I've seen some of his stuff. It's totally different. He's developed a style of his own in some of those pieces he makes—glass sculpture they call it, don't they? Something quite out of the ordinary. My aunt's got a piece, and every time I go to see her——'

Trina could bear it no more. She banged the handle of her knife on the table so that the glasses rattled, and Derek stopped in astonishment. 'Here,' he said uneasily, 'what's the matter? Have I said something?'

'Said something? Oh no,' Trina returned with heavy sarcasm. 'You haven't said a thing. Only how marvellous, and wonderful, and talented Griff Tyzak is and how lucky we are to have him. Why don't you go on and finish it? Why don't you say that the firm wouldn't stand a chance with just me in charge, that with Griff Tyzak at the helm everything would be all right? I'm sure that's what you meant to say—so why don't you just go ahead and say it?' She bit her lip, miserably aware that she was making a fool of herself and that other people were glancing round with interest. Flushing painfully, she made a vicious cut at her roast beef. 'Well, wasn't that what you meant?' she muttered.

'Well, no, it wasn't actually,' said Derek after a pause. 'Look, Trina, don't you think you're getting things a bit out of proportion? Oh, it's understandable—you've had a bad shock, losing your father like that, and it must all seem a bit overwhelming to have to take over more or less overnight. But things aren't that bad, surely? You wouldn't really have wanted to take on the responsibility all alone. And there couldn't be anyone better than Griff to give you a hand——'

'There you go again! The marvellous Griff Tyzak! What *is* it about that man? Even Dad doesn't seem to have seen through him—yet to me he seems about the most arrogant, overbearing and conceited male chauvinist pig I've ever had the misfortune to meet! Derek, he's not giving me a hand—he's just walking in and taking over. Or trying to—only I'm not letting it happen. I love Compson's and all it stands for. I'm just not *letting* him change everything.'

'Does he want to?' Derek enquired, and Trina sighed again.

'Yes! Of course he does—why else should I object? Oh, it's no use, Derek—let's not discuss it any more. I can't seem to get across to you just what it all means.'

'Well, I am trying to understand,' said Derek, knitting his brows. 'But you do have to look at it reasonably, Trina——'

'And that's just your trouble, isn't it!' she flashed. 'You've got to see everything *reasonably*! Oh——' she stopped helplessly as Derek gazed at her. 'It's no good, Derek. We're just not on the same wavelength, are we?'

'Perhaps we'd better talk about something else,' he said stiffly, and they continued their meal in silence. Trina was seething with frustration—surely her point of view wasn't so unreasonable? And now, somehow, she'd managed to hurt Derek. And if not actually sulking, he was certainly being very quiet. Oh, why did everything have to be so *difficult*?

'Look, Trina,' Derek said after a while, 'don't you really think it would be best to wait awhile before you make up your mind about all this? I mean, as I said just now, you must be under quite a bit of stress at present. Things are bound to be a bit distorted. Give it a few weeks and you'll find you see it all quite differently. You'll wonder what you were worrying about.'

Trina looked at him. He meant to be kind, she knew. It wasn't in his nature to be anything else. But did he have to be quite so patronising? Did he have to talk to her as if she were a small girl who'd broken her favourite doll? It wasn't any use saying that to him, of course. He just wouldn't know what she was talking about.

'Yes, I expect you're right, Derek,' she said quietly. 'Anyway, let's leave it for now. Let's talk about something quite different. How did you enjoy your holiday?'

'Oh, very much.' Derek's face lit up and he began to tell her about the winter holiday he had just enjoyed in Switzerland. 'Not exactly skiing, of course,' he said. 'I don't think I'd be much good at that, and I don't like to risk injuring my hands. But there were plenty of low-level walks, and the scenery is wonderful. I did quite a few sketches—thought they might come in handy for engraving some day. I've never tried anything like that before.'

'Mm, that's quite an idea.' Trina considered. 'Perhaps you could do some of those big vases with a mountain scene. It would make quite a change from wildlife—though I wouldn't like to see you stop doing those, they're beautiful.'

'I enjoy doing them.' Derek's freehand engravings of herons and kingfishers in their natural surroundings on large pieces of glass were very popular at the top end of the market. He had executed other pieces too, showing animals such as otters, badgers and hares, all of which involved lengthy study of the creature involved and a considerable knowledge of anatomy and habitat. Landscape would be a new departure for him.

Trina's tension had begun to subside and she began again to relax a little. Perhaps Derek was right—things might seem different after they'd had time to settle down. And if the other directors backed her up. . . . She glanced idly around, glad that she'd come out. It wasn't really a good idea to spend too much time alone at home. There were too many memories there.

As she let her eyes stray over the lounge, now almost full of chattering customers, she saw the street door open. A woman came in—an arrestingly beautiful woman in a silver fur jacket against which her long, shiningly auburn hair looked like spun copper. She was tall, with a haughty, imperious look about her and there was something in her bearing that drew all eyes.

Trina watched. The woman was all she had ever longed to be—poised, confident and lovely. *She* wouldn't need to fight to hold her own with a man like Griff Tyzak. She wouldn't ever need to raise her voice. She could just lift a finger and what she had commanded would be done.

The woman came a little further into the lounge and the door opened wider to admit the man she was with. And at the sight of him, Trina had to repress an exclamation. But she might have known it, she thought fatalistically. There could be only one man around here who would know such an exotic creature as this woman.

Griff Tyzak, making every other man in the place look insignificant in the dark velvet jacket that emphasised his broad shoulders and straight back, stood at the door and surveyed the lounge as if assessing its suitability to bring the lady of his choice. Then, apparently deciding that it was good enough, he led her to an armchair and made sure she was settled before going to the bar to order drinks.

He had paid for them and asked for a menu before he glanced up and caught Trina's fascinated gaze. For a moment—or was it an eternity?—he stood quite still, his dark brown eyes locked with hers. Then he gave an almost imperceptible shrug, inclined his head and continued on his way to the redhead, who was watching with narrowed eyes. Trina, feeling suddenly exhausted, tore her eyes away from him and found Derek watching her thoughtfully.

'Well, what a coincidence,' he remarked, though Trina felt sure that he was thinking something quite different. 'And I wonder who the lady is? Think he'll come over and introduce us? Or is she a part of his very private life?'

Trina woke next morning feeling dazed and heavy after a night of disturbed sleep. She had seemed to spend most of it awake, thoughts teeming through her brain, though she could recall at least two vivid dreams; one in which she had been battering on the glasshouse door, unable to get in, hearing only the clatter of the irons and the jeering laughter of men who were inside; and the other a totally incomprehensible affair in which she appeared to be Bonnie Prince Charlie, pursued across the Scottish moors by an army of Arabs in flowing robes. She woke in a panic, trying desperately to remember the name for a cairngorm brooch, and was only slightly relieved when she not only remembered it (after several attempts) but realised that it didn't really matter anyway.

Yawning, she staggered downstairs and made herself some coffee. Mrs Aston had her own flat at one end of the house and it was understood that she didn't begin her duties until nine; Trina had always enjoyed this part of the day, when she had prepared breakfast for her father and herself and they had sat together talking or reading the newspapers before setting off for the factory. Now she sat alone, shivering a little, hands clasped round the mug of coffee. She hadn't felt like eating breakfast lately, and even less like preparing it. Instead, she took an apple from the basket and munched it thoughtfully.

She still didn't know who the titian-haired beauty was who had been with Griff last night. Neither she nor Derek had ever seen her before, and it had been obvious from the glances directed at her by the other people in the hotel that she was a stranger to Bridgnorth. *Someone* would have known her if she hadn't been; it was a small town and there were few other places to dine out in the evening.

Griff had, of course, brought her over and introduced her. His expression had been quite unreadable as he stood by their table, Derek rising to his feet quickly to hold out his hand. Julia Meredith, he had introduced her as, but there was no further information. Although Julia Meredith quite clearly knew all about Trina.

'So *you're* the lady who's managed to tear Griff away from his studio,' she had drawled in an attractive, husky voice to which Trina took an immediate and unreasonable dislike. 'I'd never have thought it possible!'

Just what she'd meant by that, Trina wasn't sure, but she managed a smile and corrected her.

'It's not me that's the attraction, I'm afraid. Griff's been lucky enough to acquire a rather good job with us——' she made it sound as if she were employing him, and saw his eyebrows rise slightly. 'But we naturally don't want to interfere with his own work. He can go back to his studio at any time.' And how! she thought, wishing that he'd do just that. But both he and Julia were looking amused now and she knew that she had only sounded childish. After all, Julia obviously knew exactly what the position was. It was silly to try to pretend anything else.

'Oh, I'm sure he'll manage to combine the two,' Julia was saying lightly. 'Griff's a very capable man, wouldn't you say? I should think there's very little he can't manage.' She let her china-blue eyes move slowly over the powerful figure beside her. 'At least, that's my experience.'

And no doubt you've had plenty of experience where Griff's concerned, Trina thought cattily. And wondered just what that sudden sharp pain was that she felt then, somewhere in the region of her breastbone.

'Why don't you join us?' Derek asked suddenly, and Trina glanced at him and noticed with some surprise the admiration with which he was regarding Julia Meredith. Well, there was no reason to suppose he'd be immune—even Trina had to admit the other woman's undoubted attraction. But surely she was several years older than Derek—probably in her early thirties, Trina guessed, though her skin was flawless and glowing, and her hair had the fine softness of a baby's. There was a sheen of sophistication about her, however, that didn't seem to come much before the late twenties, and Trina felt suddenly gauche and immature, her clothes arty and flamboyant beside the simple elegance of Julia's plain black jersey dress. She glanced quickly at Griff but received no help from him, and when she spoke her voice was high and brittle.

'Yes, why don't you, that would be lovely,' she said falsely. 'Only we shan't be here long. We were just going to have a coffee before leaving, weren't we, Derek?' She glared at his surprised face and cut short the objection she knew he was about to make on not having had dessert yet. 'Slimming, you know,' she added weakly.

'Oh, I do understand,' Julia exclaimed sympathetically. 'I used to be just the same—such a relief to get out of the puppy-fat stage. But I think they've already decided which table we're to have—that nice private one over in the corner. So if you'll excuse us, we'll go and claim it. Don't want to confuse the management, do we?' She turned to Derek and smiled warmly at him. 'It's been so nice to meet you, Derek. I hope we'll be seeing lots more of each other in the future. I'm sure we will!' The way she tucked her hand into Griff's arm then was positively possessive. 'Come along, darling, we haven't even glanced at the menu yet.'

Trina watched them settle themselves at their table, Julia shrugging out of her fur jacket—must be mink, she thought—which was borne respectfully away by the waiter. That jersey dress hadn't come from a chain store either—if Julia had had any change out of a hundred and fifty pounds, Trina would have been surprised. And that was probably a conservative estimate.

'Attractive, isn't she?' Derek observed, following her glance and catching a brief but dazzling smile from Julia. 'Wonder where Griff found her?'

'I wouldn't like to guess,' Trina said shortly. 'Derek, can we go now? I honestly don't want a dessert.'

'But I thought you said we were having coffee. . . .' Derek caught her eye and seemed to realise at last that she was serious. 'Oh, all right. But it seems rather early. Still, I suppose you're probably tired. I'll take you straight home and you can have an early night. I expect you need it.'

Why not just come straight out and say I look

haggard? Trina thought bitterly. Especially beside Julia Meredith! Oh, hell—why had Griff had to bring her here tonight, of all nights? Just when she was beginning to relax a little. She pulled her brightly-coloured jacket around her, feeling suddenly that its gaiety was crude and unsuitable. The evening had definitely not been a success.

Neither did it improve once they were out of the hotel. It had begun to sleet and they had to walk far enough to the car to get cold and damp, although Trina noticed at once that Griff's Volvo was parked immediately outside. The roads were treacherous and Derek, a cautious driver at the best of times, reached no more than a crawl all the way back to Compson House. By the time they got there, Trina was almost at screaming point.

'Would you like to come in for a coffee?' she asked through set teeth, not sure what she wanted him to answer but knowing that whatever it was, it would be wrong.

Derek considered. 'No, I don't think I will, if you don't mind,' he said at last. 'It really is a filthy night and it's getting worse. I think I'd better get straight home before I'm stranded.'

Trina looked at him. They had never been more than affectionate friends, ending their evenings with a kiss, but suddenly she wanted something more. She longed to be held in strong arms, kissed with passion and meaning, her emotions set free to be swept away on a frenzied tide of desire. Dimly she knew that only in this way would that strange, heavy pain somewhere deep inside her be assuaged. And whom else should she turn to but Derek? They had known each other since their schooldays, shared so much. She had, more than once, thought of sharing her life with him.

'Derek,' she whispered, moving closer to him and lifting her face to his, 'please come in for a while. It doesn't really matter if you get stranded, does it—so long as it's here. I'm so lonely, Derek.'

He looked at her. In the dim light of the car she

could see his face, surprised and disconcerted. Before he could speak, she wound her arms round his neck and began to kiss him—pressing her lips against his in a desperate attempt to kindle some passion both in him and in herself. But there was no response, only the movement of recoil as Derek shifted away from her and reached his hands up to her shoulders to push her gently away.

'Not now, Trina,' he murmured. 'It's not really the right time, is it? You're still upset, overwrought. I can't take advantage of you now.' He smiled at her. 'You go on in and get Mrs Aston to make you a cup of Horlicks and a hot-water bottle. Don't let's do anything we might regret later.'

Trina stared at him. Her feelings now were even more confused; frustration, disappointment, anger and—oddly—relief, all surged like a maelstrom inside her. But none of them could be expressed to Derek. Kindly and placid, he just wouldn't have any idea what she meant, putting it all down to tiredness and a backlash of grief over her father's death. And perhaps he was right at that, she acknowledged, feeling suddenly drained and exhausted. Perhaps it really would all seem different in the morning, as one of her nannies had been wont to say over some childish crisis. In any case, the relief she needed wasn't going to come from Derek and it really wasn't any use blaming him for that.

'I'm sorry, Derek,' she said dully, opening the car door. 'You're right—I'm really rather worn out. I'll see you tomorrow, at the factory.'

'You have a good long sleep,' he advised. 'That's what you need. You've been overdoing things, Trina, and really there isn't any need. Not when you've got Gr——'

Trina slammed the door before he could finish, and ran through the sleet to the steps. She turned and waved, because she didn't want to hurt Derek; then she opened the door and slipped inside.

She hadn't even thanked him for taking her out, she remembered as she leaned back against the wall, blessedly alone at last. But Derek wouldn't mind. He'd know she'd enjoyed it.

Only she hadn't, had she? Trina climbed slowly up the stairs, forgetting about Horlicks and hot-water bottles—Mrs Aston would have turned on her electric blanket anyway. She hadn't enjoyed the evening at all—it had been wrong, out of key, from start to finish. And the strength and support she'd looked for from Derek hadn't been forthcoming after all He'd never even realised she needed them. She wondered suddenly how Griff and Julia Meredith were enjoying *their* evening. And whether they would afterwards share a late-night drink in some warm and intimate room.

And just what else they would share together. . . .

Trina finished her apple and poured another mug of coffee. Her head still felt thick and muzzy, and she needed to be able to think clearly for that board meeting Griff had called for this morning. Frowning, she tried to marshal her arguments against change; not that she had much to worry about, she was sure. The others would be bound to back her. But one never knew—Griff had that inexplicable charisma, that magnetism that drew people to him, and she was quite certain that he would use every ounce of it to get his own way. He always had been able to charm the birds off the trees, she thought bitterly.

With this in mind, she dressed carefully, putting on a suit of soft, misty-blue tweed that brought out the gold lights in her hair, wearing under the jacket a high-necked sweater of thin jersey in a toning shade. She considered herself carefully in the mirror. Make-up, not too lavishly applied, hid the tiredness around her eyes, and she looked both feminine and businesslike. Quite capable of holding down the job of Managing Director, she thought determinedly, and set off to the garage to get her car out.

Things began to go wrong at once. The up-and-over door had stuck and she struggled with it nearly five minutes in the freezing wind, her hair blowing irritatingly round her eyes and her suit getting increasingly damp in the sleet that was still falling. At last she managed to free it and it flew up with a jerk, breaking two fingernails as it went and showering Trina with droplets of icy water from the bottom. Cursing, she brushed the drops from her suit and scuttled into the garage, opening the car door with frozen fingers. It was only to be expected after that, that the car would refuse to start.

It was half an hour before Trina, growing more agitated every minute, finally admitted defeat and got out again. Presumably the battery was flat, and she knew that by now her repeated efforts to get the engine started would have flooded the carburettor. Grudging the time, but knowing it would have to be done, she put the battery on charge and went back into the house for the keys of her father's car.

'Goodness me, I thought you'd gone!' Mrs Aston exclaimed, encountering her in the hall. 'Whatever's happened? You look frozen to death!'

'Car wouldn't start.' Trina looked at herself in the hall mirror. The suit seemed to have survived all right, thank goodness, but her hair was a mess and her make-up was definitely the worse for wear. She glanced at her watch. The meeting was due to begin in half an hour—it would be a rush to get there, in this weather, and although she knew they wouldn't start without her she didn't really want to arrive at her first board meeting late. But then neither did she want to arrive looking dishevelled and untidy. She bit her lip in an agony of indecision, then made up her mind and ran up to her bedroom. After all, the weather was excuse enough for lateness—and her father's car was capable of going faster than her little Metro, as well as being large enough to cut itself a swathe through other traffic. Trina didn't normally approve of such bullying tactics, but she was beginning to see why people employed them!

She arrived at the factory at last, relieved that nothing else had gone wrong—a burst water-main, landslip and multiple accident would each have been in character for this depressing and unpleasant winter's morning, she thought bleakly—and hastily parked the big Jaguar outside the offices. Then, trying to hurry while looking simultaneously casual and at ease, she walked through the doors and made for the boardroom, stopped outside it to give her hair and suit a final quick check.

Everything seemed to be all right. And a glance at her watch showed that she was no more than seven minutes late. She might not even be the last arrival.

She took a deep breath, told herself sternly to stop feeling like a child presenting herself at the headmistress's study, and opened the door.

There was no sound from within. No hum of conversation, broken off as she entered, no scraping of chairs or laughter. And it was easy enough, as Trina stood baffled in the doorway, to see why.

The boardroom was empty. The long table shone with the polishing of years, the chairs were ranged neatly around it. But there was nobody there. The room was completely deserted.

Trina blinked and rubbed her eyes. *Now* what had happened? Had she mistaken the date, or the time? Was she so late that they'd had the meeting and dispersed already? No—that couldn't be true. Even now, it was only just after ten. And however bad the weather, *someone* should have arrived. Robert Nicklin, for instance, lived within walking distance. And so did one or two of the others.

Trina heard footsteps hurrying along the corridor, and turned quickly. 'Jean! What's going on—where are the others?'

'Oh, there you are, Trina.' Jean had known her for years and had been a tower of strength since William Compson had died. 'I'm sorry we couldn't let you know, but the board meeting's been cancelled.'

'Cancelled?' Trina stared at her. 'Cancelled by whom?'

'Mr Tyzak cancelled it. He rang in quite early—said

he wouldn't be able to make it after all, he had some rather important business to attend to. He'll let us know when it's convenient.'

'Oh, he'll let us know, will he?' Trina exclaimed, forgetting that she'd never wanted this meeting and had been awake half the night worrying about it. 'Well, that *is* good of him, I must say! And suppose it just doesn't happen to be convenient to me? Did he mention that, I wonder?'

'Well, no.' Jean looked embarrassed and faintly surprised. 'No, I thought you'd probably work it out between you. I'm sorry, Trina. Was it really important? Mr Tyzak didn't seem to think it was.'

'Well, he should know—he called it.' Trina turned away impatiently. 'No, it doesn't really matter, Jean, not in the least. It's just that I've had a foul time getting here and it's a bit annoying to find everything cancelled without any reference to me.'

'I'm sorry, I really am.' Jean's homely face was full of concern. 'We did try to ring you, but there was no answer. Perhaps your phone's out of order—I wouldn't be surprised, in this weather. This wet sleet clogs up the junction boxes, or something.'

'Oh lord, I suppose that's it. I'd better get on to the telephone people. Or perhaps you'd do that for me, Jean.'

'Yes, of course. And I'll get you some coffee, too. You look really worn out.' The older woman bustled off towards her office, and Trina leaned against the wall for a moment before following her.

Worn out already—at ten in the morning? What was the matter with her—she'd always had inexhaustible energy! Now, it seemed that the first thing everyone noticed about her was how tired she looked.

Slowly she made her way to her own office and sat down, sifting apathetically through the morning's mail. What had caused Griff to cancel the meeting? she wondered dully. It must have been something that had happened since last night, since he'd made no mention of it then.

A picture flashed into her mind then of Julia Meredith, beautiful and assured, tucking her arm possessively into Griff's before leading him away to the secluded little table in the corner. It wasn't too hard to guess at what might have happened to make him reluctant to travel in to the office that morning. Other important business to attend to indeed! Her lip curled with scorn. Well, that certainly made Griff's position as regards Compson Crystal quite clear. As clear as—well, as crystal, in fact. But the pun did nothing to amuse her. Instead, she felt sick at heart as she sat gazing sightlessly across the desk and trying not to see pictures of Griff and Julia together, attending to their 'important business'.

Damn Griff Tyzak! *Damn* him!

CHAPTER FOUR

GRIFF didn't appear at the glassworks that day, neither did he come in on the next. Trina stayed at her desk, working through the mail and asking Robert Nicklin for advice when she wasn't sure. Jean, too, was helpful with her knowledge of so much of the Managing Director's work, and between them they kept the in-tray reasonably empty and the out-tray fairly active. The pending tray, however, began to pile up worryingly high, and Trina was reminded of her father's declaration after a particularly harassing week that he was going to name it the 'Too Difficult' tray. It wasn't that there was anything she couldn't have dealt with alone if she'd had total authority, she told herself as she looked at it resentfully on the Friday evening. It was just that with Griff holding responsibility on equal terms, her hands were tied. Although she wasn't at all sure that she would let that count if she hadn't heard from him by Monday. He couldn't go off into the blue and expect everything to stop and wait for his return!

And just where was he, anyway? There had been no word from him since the phone call cancelling the board meeting. Thankful as she was not to have him breathing down her neck, Trina was still irritated by his continued absence. It really wasn't good enough! Either he was joint managing director or he wasn't, and if he was then he ought to be taking his position seriously. He had appeared to be doing just that a few days ago, with all his talk about branching out into colour and new styles. Now, he seemed to have simply lost interest.

Trina shrugged and turned off her office light. Jean was finishing some typing in the outer office and looked up as Trina came through, shrugging into her duffle coat. Trina paused by her desk for a moment, suddenly reluctant to go. It was a warm, cosy world here, a world she knew and felt secure with. Outside it was cold and dark, and home was a big, lonely house. Mrs Aston was there, of course, but Mrs Aston had her own busy private life; she had her own flat, her knitting and tapestry work, her favourite TV programmes and several outside interests such as the Women's Institute and the church choir. She had a good many friends in the district too, as well as several relations, and would often be out visiting them or having them to visit her.

'I shan't be long finishing these letters,' Jean remarked, fitting another sheet of paper in her typewriter. 'You go along and have a nice weekend. Don't do too much, now.'

'There's not much to do,' Trina answered, and then, hearing the dreary note in her voice, added with a quick smile: 'Mrs Aston seems to cope with everything. But I expect I'll potter about in the garden and go for a walk if the weather's fine.'

She went out into the cold air, feeling the raw wind bite at her cheeks, and shivered. Go for a walk, she thought—the weather would have to be a lot better than this to tempt her out! An afternoon by the library fire with a good book and some pleasant music playing would be much more to her taste. But somehow the prospect didn't charm her. Such an afternoon could be cosy and intimate spent in the company of someone you loved, she thought. Alone—well, it was no better and no worse than any other way of passing the time, and that was all that could be said about it.

Mrs Aston had made a steak and kidney pie which Trina ate alone—she did quite often eat with the housekeeper, but this was Women's Institute night, so she was left to sit by herself in the small breakfast-room she and her father had used as a dining-room when they were alone, watching television as she ate. The hot food was comforting, but she did little more than pick at it; the apple charlotte which followed seemed dull and uninteresting, and she had only a few mouthfuls before pushing her plate aside. She carried the dishes through to the kitchen, washed them up and took the coffee-pot to the library where the fire was burning cheerfully.

At least she could do something useful. There had been no time to do any of her own design work that week, and she was anxious to develop a new range which could be put into production later in the year, ready for the Christmas market. 'Winter' it was to be called, the forerunner of a series depicting the seasons, and she had already begun on some ideas involving snowflakes and bare, windswept trees. There was Derek's idea about the mountain scenery, too; perhaps that could be incorporated somewhere.

Time passed more quickly once she had begun work, and Trina sat at her desk until almost eleven. Then, suddenly aware that she felt stiff and tired and that the fire had gone out, she dropped her pencil and stretched her cramped fingers. Well, she was tired enough now— surely tonight she would sleep?

But she didn't. Tired as she was when she slipped into bed, sleep seemed determined to elude her and she spent another uncomfortable night, never quite sure whether she was asleep or awake, her thoughts teeming like ants yet as elusive as moths. And when she did sleep, her dreams were full of anxiety and a sense of hurrying to get somewhere that she knew she could never reach in time; a sense of being cruelly, callously left behind.

Sunday dawned bright and frosty. Trina woke late, having fallen into a deep sleep towards dawn, and decided to waste no time before going for the walk she had promised herself. Saturday had been cold and grey, with an icy wind and tiny, hard snowflakes in the air; she had spent the morning in the garden, raking up the last of the leaves and the afternoon in the kitchen with Mrs Aston, learning to make bread. The daytime hours out of the way, she had then settled to some more designing in the library.

It was odd how time had become suddenly so difficult to cope with, she thought as she dressed in a warm sweater and trousers and went downstairs to have a quick breakfast of porridge before going out. She had never had any trouble before; there had never seemed to be enough hours in the day, or days in the week. Now, unless she was at the factory, time seemed to stretch endlessly ahead of her, the hours lonely and arid.

Yet it couldn't all be due to her father's death. Close as they had been, they had each had their own interests and there had been many weekends when Trina, caught up in her own social whirl, had scarcely seen him. Just what had she done on those busy weekends? she wondered now. Nothing that seemed really worth doing.

The sun was sparkling on frost-rimmed grass and branches as she set out, a bar of chocolate and an apple in her jacket pocket. Ice on puddles crunched underfoot and the air smelt crisp and spicy. As she made her way from the lawns surrounding the house to the copse she saw that the dead bracken was outlined in a thick fur of frost, each frond like a huge white feather. The theme was repeated in the silver birch trees, their delicate mesh of leafless branches like glittering filigree against the pale robin's-egg sky.

Trina walked steadily, taking note of each tiny new discovery and thinking of her designs. This was what she loved best about her job; the translation of what she found beautiful into something that everyone could enjoy; something equally beautiful, in a different medium. Derek ought to be here to see this, she thought; his freehand engraving was just what could express most accurately the delight that lay all around her. It was strange that such artistic sensitivity should exist in a man who had no idea at all about the feelings a woman might have, the emotions that could beset and confuse her.

Griff Tyzak's face came into her mind then and she wondered whether he would be any more understanding—provided one was on good terms with him to start with, of course! As she herself had been once. She thought of the days when, as a young teenager, she had come into the glasshouse and watched him at work. In the middle twenties then, he had appeared to her like some kind of Greek god, his physique approaching

perfection as he worked the glass, swinging his iron to
lengthen the glowing lump, his muscles gleaming in the
red light of the furnace. He had always worn his thick
black hair on the long side, and she had loved the way
it flopped over his face, so that he had to toss his head
like an angry young bull to flick it back into place. But
there had been nothing else to suggest anger; he had
been totally absorbed in his work, marvering the glass
and blowing it into shape, his breath coming from deep
in his diaphragm so that it seemed to be without effort,
with no sign of the puffed-out cheeks that could be seen
in old pictures of glassblowers. Yet the metal at the end
of his iron would expand like a Christmas balloon,
taking on exactly the shape he wanted; long and thin,
elegantly tapered, chubby and pear-shaped or perfectly
spherical.

They had never had another blower with the talent
Griff had shown. Even Trevor, the finest craftsman in
the works now, an artist in his own right, had never
managed to attain quite the heights that Griff had so
easily scaled. Once again, Trina relived the hurt and
disappointment she had known when her father had
told her Griff was leaving; once again she felt the anger
that had been her only way of expressing it.

'*Leaving?*' she had echoed unbelievingly. 'But why?
You *can't* let him leave, Daddy!'

'Why not?' William Compson countered with
amusement, and Trina hesitated and floundered,
unwilling to say what she only dimly felt, that if Griff
would only stay until she was grown up she was sure
he'd love her as she loved him. . . . No, she couldn't say
that. Nobody would take her seriously—a schoolgirl of
fifteen. Her father might even consider that if she really
felt like that it would probably be best if Griff were
encouraged to leave!

Instead, she said lamely: 'He's our best man, Daddy.
Nobody else can blow glass like he does. We've trained
him—we *need* him.'

Her father had raised his eyebrows slightly at that
'we', but she knew he was pleased that she identified so

strongly with the firm. But he'd merely told her that Griff's potential was greater than they could cope with at Compson's just now, and it would be wrong to hold him back. 'Later on, we might be able to extend ourselves to embrace his talent,' he'd said. 'Just now, it's better for him to have his own small studio where he can experiment and develop his style.'

There'd been sense in his words, but Trina hadn't wanted to see it. She had continued to look on Griff's departure as a betrayal. Develop his style, indeed! What was wrong with the style they had evolved at Compson Crystal—a style that was world-famous, held everywhere in high regard? And the things they made there were functional, too. Tableware that could be used with pleasure, enhancing both their setting and the foods and wines they contained. Not mere ornaments, to be glanced at now and then and dusted every day. Not clever-clever 'friggers', the glass ships in bottles and elaborate birds in cages that had been made for fun when nobody was looking and sold discreetly to visitors at the factory door. There were plenty of those about and everyone enjoyed playing with the raw material to see just what could be done with it, but it would never make a serious line. Not at Compson Crystal, anyway.

She was up on the Edge now, walking along the narrow ridge from which she could see all over the surrounding countryside—the chimneys and towers of Stourbridge on her right, with the great conurbations of Dudley, Birmingham and Wolverhampton stretching away beyond. And to her left the rolling green hills of southern Shropshire, with the brown humps of the Clee hills topped with their white, mushroom-like radomes.

The Edge was almost like a dividing line between the two kinds of landscape, peacefully rural and bustlingly urban. Yet all this area had been part of the industrial scene, particularly during the nineteenth century when the ironmasters had grown prosperous on the earth's riches. Her own great-grandfather had been just such a man, secure enough in his fortune to buy the failing glassworks and inject new life into it. If he hadn't done

that, where would she be today? Designing stainless
steel knives and forks? Or doing something completely
different, never really knowing her own capabilities?

It was strange that Griff had so suddenly absented
himself from the factory. Trina couldn't help wondering
where he was and what he was doing. She was quite
sure that the elegant Julia had a good deal to do with it.
She was clearly very much in Griff's confidence—
perhaps they were even going to get married. Trina
shivered, feeling again that odd little pain inside. Well,
they were welcome to each other—provided they didn't
try, between them, to take over Compson Crystal. She
had a feeling that Julia wasn't the type to be satisfied by
playing second string. She would want to be First Lady
as far as the factory was concerned—and where would
that leave Trina?

Out in the cold, she thought miserably. Back in the
design office. Well, that wouldn't be too bad in itself—
she'd always been happy there and could admit to
herself that it suited her a lot better than administra-
tion—but not if it meant handing over control to Griff
and his lady friend, whoever she might be. Oh no—that
was *quite* out of the question!

Surprisingly for a fine Sunday, the Edge was almost
deserted, only a few people passing Trina as she
wandered along, warm now with the exercise. She
followed the path below the Edge for a while, through
trees still outlined in white, with spiders' webs like lace
handkerchiefs slung between their branches, and
stopped for a moment under a shelf of red rock. She
had always loved to come here as a child, with her
father; the cave that had been partly hewn, partly
formed by natural causes, under its frowning brow, had
been her especial delight.

And people had actually lived here, almost within
living memory, she thought, ducking her head to creep
in through the wide opening that made a picture
window looking out towards the western sky. Here and
in the other caves and rock dwellings that peppered the
area. Well, in good weather they probably had a point.

There wouldn't be a much nicer spot to live than here, with this wonderful view, and you didn't need planning permission for a cave. On the other hand, she was glad she would be returning to a solid house that evening, with a log fire to sit by in a comfortable armchair.

She walked on along the path. Her objective was, as it had to be when on the Edge, the high, fortress-like knoll below the very end of the ridge which had been honeycombed into a labyrinth of rock-dwellings—you could hardly call them caves, for they had been improved and shaped until the entire rock was a warren of small rooms and passages, rising like a great red anthill out of the earth. The dwellings had been constructed on several levels; Trina had been here once when an outing of schoolchildren had paid a visit, swarming over the rock, popping in and out of doors and windows until the whole thing took on the aspect of a nursery rhyme. The old woman who lived in a shoe, she'd thought, smiling at the comical sight. She would have been thrilled with Holy Austin Rock.

Today it was deserted and silent. But as Trina approached she had an odd feeling that she wasn't alone—a prickling of the spine that told her someone was watching her. Uneasily, she stopped and glanced around. She saw no one and moved on, still unsure. And then he stepped out of the undergrowth, straight ahead of her, the low winter sunshine full on his face so that the black hair clustered round his head like a nimbus and his dark eyes flashed like deep brown gemstones in the clear light.

'Griff!' Trina gasped, and the frosty world swung about her. 'What on earth are *you* doing here?' And, dizzy with the shock, she put out a hand to steady herself.

She felt herself drawn into strong arms, held against a broad wall of a chest. She could feel the pounding of his heart deep inside, and at the same moment she knew that her own heartbeats had quickened. His body was firm against hers from shoulder to toe, every contour testifying to his virile masculinity, and she clung to him as if to one of the rocks that surrounded them, feeling inexplicably that here was the security and comfort that she craved, the solid basis that had been missing from her life even without her knowing it.

Griff slid one hand up her back, his fingers sliding beneath the anorak and sweater so that she felt them, warm and vibrant, almost against her skin. With his other hand he lifted her chin, tilting her face towards him and looking down at her with grave eyes.

'Griff?' she whispered, her lips scarcely moving to form the word, and as if it were a signal he uttered a deep groan and held her even closer against him as his mouth came down to cover hers. The dizziness swept over Trina once more, swinging her, it seemed, between earth and sky as Griff's lips opened hers with a tenderness she wouldn't have believed in, his mouth making an exploration that drew a response she hadn't known she could make. She whimpered in her throat, her fingers clutching convulsively at his back and shoulders before finding their way up to tangle in the hair that grew thickly down the back of his neck. Quivering in his arms, she let her body move against his, wishing that there was less between them, their sweaters and jackets thick encumbrances that nevertheless could not muffle all sensation. Excitement ran like tongues of fire through her body, making her stomach tingle and her legs tremble, so that she would have fallen if he had not been holding her so close.

'This is no good,' he muttered at last. 'Let's get into the rock—where we can be private. Oh, Trina—Trina. . . .'

Trina felt her legs move automatically as Griff, still supporting her in his arms, led her towards the great red rock. Still dazed, she lifted her head and saw that the world was still there, surprisingly unchanged; the hoar-frost still sparkling on the trees and bushes, brilliant flashes of diamond brightness striking from the crystals of ice as the sun's rays glanced across them.

Griff drew her into the shelter of a roughly-hewn doorway. It was like a small living-room inside, grooves in the wall showing where hinges had held an oak door or curtains had hung across the window-gap. There was even a fireplace scooped out of one wall, with a tunnelled chimney leading up to the outside.

Trina had no time to notice more than this before Griff was kissing her again and once more she was whirled away into a tempest of desire, her whole body caught up in the one fierce longing that battered about her like a storm, tearing at her heart and mind so that nothing else mattered, nothing but this . . . and this . . . and this. . . . Her mind closed itself to all rational thought, spinning her into a vortex of passion from which there was only one escape, only one way out; and as Griff lowered her gently to the rough sandy floor she consciously abandoned herself to the rapture that must surely follow, the consequences forgotten as an instinct as old and as powerful as time took subtle charge and the pulse of an ageless enchantment beat inexorably through them both.

'Here it is,' called a voice from outside. 'Just like in the picture, look! Imagine people actually *living* here!'

Trina jolted back to reality and looked up at Griff with suddenly dilated eyes. With a muttered curse, he jerked her to her feet and pulled her rumpled sweater down to cover skin that had somehow become bare. He ran a shaking hand through his dark hair and his mouth twisted ruefully as he met her agonised gaze.

'Close thing,' he muttered as the voices came closer, and taking her by the hand he stepped outside, looking for all the world like an innocent sightseer. Trina followed, still trembling and convinced that anyone could see at a glance exactly what she had been doing. Not that she was quite sure herself, she admitted wryly. What had happened had been so quick, so unexpected and so entirely outside any of her previous experience that it could almost have been a dream. Except that dreams didn't usually leave you feeling bruised and shaken and totally disorientated.

'This *is* the Holy Austin Rock, isn't it?' the man outside asked as they emerged. He was standing with a woman and two children, staring up at it and referring to a book in his hand.

'Yes, that's right,' Griff answered pleasantly. 'Interesting, isn't it? Seems strange to think of people living there, but actually it's quite snug inside.' He turned to Trina. 'Isn't it, darling?'

To her relief, she wasn't required to answer this. The strangers, having found themselves a guide, were peppering Griff with questions and seemed hardly to notice Trina as she stood there, her hand still lost in Griff's. How long was it since the rock had been used? What kind of people lived there—gipsies? Was it the only such rock in the area or were there more? Could you go and see them?

Trina was surprised at the knowledge Griff showed. Yes, he answered, there were more and some of them were quite easy to find, others had become lost and forgotten, smothered in brambles and bushes. There were a few hewn-out dwellings in Wolverley, he told them, where the old ironmasters had housed their workers. But here on the Edge, in Holy Austin Rock, people had lived until the 1950's, reluctant to move out until the Council insisted, and then—so people said— they had missed the 'healthy' red sandstone walls and died within a short time.

'They were all probably quite old by then, so one mustn't read too much into it,' he added, smiling. 'But they obviously liked living here—and they built on extensions here and there too, see? One of them used to be a café, so it was a livelihood as well as a home.'

The family listened, fascinated by this glimpse into housing conditions in rural Staffordshire and Worcestershire, and then the children scampered into the rock to explore its honeycomb of passages and rooms. The parents smiled at Griff and Trina and thanked them before following.

'Well, that could have been worse,' Griff commented as he led Trina away along the path, still holding her hand. 'But I think we'd better find a more private place before we continue our—er—meeting, don't you?'

His words brought Trina back to reality with a jolt. She stopped dead and stared up at him, trying ineffectually to pull her hand away. All at once panic overtook her; he didn't mean to let her go, he was going to force her—and she jerked frantically at his hand, trying to free her fingers and feeling tears of desperation prick at her eyelids.

'What's the matter? What is it?' Griff kept a firm hold on her hand, his brown eyes searching her face, drawing her on along the track.

'Griff, let go! I can't—I don't know what got into me—it mustn't happen again——' They were out of sight of the rock now and she stopped again, trying to free herself with both hands now.

'Mustn't it? But why not? Don't tell me you didn't like it!' His tone was mocking as he pulled her closer, and Trina struggled wildly. He mustn't kiss her again— mustn't touch her in that intimate way that sent her senses reeling and closed her mind to reason. 'You enjoyed that as much as I did, Trina,' he went on positively. 'So what's the problem?'

Trina was beginning to recover from the effect of his kisses and feel blessedly angry. She stopped trying to pull her hand away and brushed her feathery hair back from her face with the other. Green eyes flashed as she faced him and her voice was cutting.

'*I* don't have any problem,' she told him. '*You're* the one with the problem—you seem to think that a few minutes in your arms and I'll be begging for more! Well, I'm sorry, but it's really not like that at all. All right, it was quite pleasant——' she was proud of that 'quite pleasant'—'but I really don't want to repeat the experience. Once is enough, thank you very much.'

Griff stared at her. His eyes were like narrow chips of flint and his breath came quickly. A tenseness stiffened his jaw. Trina watched him warily. She wasn't at all sure that it had worked—this rejection of his lovemaking, the impression she had tried to give that it had meant almost nothing to her, no more than a few moments' pleasure to pass the time.

But it was vitally important that it *did* work. Griff must never, never know just how he really did make her feel. He must never realise the power he could so easily wield over her—and would wield, once she had allowed him to take possession of her emotions and her body as he had so nearly done only half an hour earlier. Dimly, she knew that her only hope lay in keeping him at more than arm's length. She didn't analyse exactly what she meant by 'hope'—she only knew that her feelings for Griff, combined with her reaction to his return and the manner of it, left her confused and frightened. She couldn't risk going any further.

'You're obviously a connoisseur of men and their attentions,' Griff said at last, and the tinge of scorn in his voice stung her. She lifted one shoulder indifferently.

'I doubt if I'm quite as experienced as you.' She wasn't going to tell him that she had hardly known any men—only Derek, and his attentions had gone no further than a casual kiss of goodnight after an evening out. She remembered the other night, when her own pent-up feelings had made her try to rouse him—*Griff* wouldn't have needed any encouragement, she thought wryly, and wondered why she had wanted to rouse Derek yet felt so afraid of Griff. Perhaps it was because she felt she could control the one—whereas the other would sweep her into a world of which she knew nothing, which frightened her even as she responded.

'Well, all right.' Griff let go of her hand abruptly. 'I've never forced any woman yet—never had to, I may say.' Meaning that most women fell at his feet like cut flowers, she thought cynically. 'But I think you'll come round, little Trina. There's an electricity between us like a high-voltage cable, and it's direct current too. You can't pretend you don't feel it just as much as I do. You can't ignore that kind of thing, Trina. Not when you're in such close contact as we're going to be.'

'Oh, so we *are* going to be in close contact?' Trina was thankful for the excuse to steer the conversation in another direction. 'I'd begun to wonder. You called a board meeting the other morning, remember? Yet when I arrived I found that you'd phoned in to say you were too busy, and we haven't seen hide nor hair of you since.'

'And does that bother you?' he murmured. 'Trina, you're welcome to see all the hide and hair you like at any time. . . . But as for the board meeting—well, it wasn't that urgent, was it? And the chance came up of a cottage to rent until I find myself something more permanent. I had to make a quick decision, and having done that it seemed common sense to move in straightaway. Wasn't unreasonable, was it?'

'No . . . I suppose not.' Trina was taken aback. She'd hoped that Griff would have stayed on in Herefordshire for a bit longer, leaving her in control of the factory. Now it seemed that he was going to be there immediately. She wouldn't even have a chance of consolidating her own position before he began trying to take over.

'Where is the cottage?' she asked, more for something to say than because she was really interested.

'Not far from here. Quite close to you, in fact—that little place about a mile from your gate, set back from the road—know it? Sandstone built, with a thatched roof.'

'Where old Major Wright used to live?'

'That's it. I heard it was empty and snapped it up. It'll do fine until I've made some more permanent plans.'

'And what are they likely to be?' As if she didn't know!

'Why, to settle near the glassworks, of course. I can't work efficiently if I'm not on the spot. I'm sorry to be leaving Herefordshire, of course—but I won't be too far away to slip back if I'm needed.'

'So you're keeping on the studio?' They walked on along the track. The frost had disappeared now except in shady places, though ice still glittered in the puddles.

'Oh yes,' he said as if there had been no question of

it, 'I'll be keeping the studio. Tyzak Glass is making quite a name for itself now, you know.'

'It's a pity you can't be satisfied with it, in that case,' Trina said recklessly. 'You wouldn't want to come muscling in at Compson Crystal then!'

Griff stopped. His hands gripped her arms, fingers biting into the soft flesh even through the jacket and sweater she wore, and he turned her towards him. His face was pale with anger, and Trina shivered. Oh, what chance did she have against this man? Physical strength was the only thing he knew to get his own way—and he had so much of it.

'I hope you won't repeat that, Trina,' he grated. 'Just remember this—I never came "muscling in" on Compson Crystal. I came by invitation—*your father's* invitation. For which he probably had very good reason, and I'm beginning to understand only too well just what that reason was.'

'Oh yes?' Terrified though she was, Trina wasn't going to let him see it. She raised her chin, green eyes meeting glittering bronze, and her voice was resolute. 'And maybe you'd like to tell me your theories about Dad's very good reasons? I'd like to hear them.'

'All right—you asked for it.' He gave her a shake with each word as he spoke, slowly and clearly. 'You are—without doubt—the most spoiled little bitch it's ever been my misfortune to encounter. Talk about Daddy's darling! Oh, I don't blame him entirely—it was natural, in the circumstances, to want to give you anything you wanted. But my God, didn't you just take it, with both hands! You've had life all your own way, Trina Compson, and you don't really see why it shouldn't go on like that, do you? The little princess becomes queen of the whole caboosh! I can just imagine what you thought—the plans you made for running everything just the way *you* wanted it, without giving a thought to anyone else. Do you know something? In good times, the works would have gone bankrupt in five years with you at the helm. With things as they are now, you could do it in less than two! No wonder your father made that condition! He saw all too clearly what you were like—he knew damned well what would happen if he didn't get someone in to stop you taking a headlong gallop into ruin. And that's why he chose me—because he knew I'd see what needed doing and make sure it was done. He knew I wouldn't kowtow to you. He knew I could control both you and the firm, and make a darned good job of both!'

He stopped, breathing hard, but evidently with plenty more to say. But Trina didn't wait to find out what it was. Furiously angry, she wrenched herself free and stood with fists clenched at her sides, glaring at him, her cheeks flushed and her eyes flashing green fire.

'Oh, so you can, can you? You really think you can "control" me, as if I were a puppy? You say "sit" and I sit, "stay" and I stay? And you really believe that Dad made that condition just so that you could do it? Oh, you do have a lot to learn, Griff Tyzak! You have a lot to learn about me and a lot more to learn about yourself. I'm not just a naughty little girl to be shown how to behave—I'm an adult, a grown woman, and I don't have to take that kind of treatment from *anyone*! I've grown up with Compson Crystal, I know the factory and the men and I know what Dad wanted for them. I've worked there ever since I left art college, I'm chief designer, and I didn't get to that position just because of my name. I got it because I'm *good*——'

'Which doesn't automatically equip you for the position of Managing Director——' he cut in, and Trina tossed her hair back, infuriated.

'Of course it doesn't—but I must be at least as good as you, who haven't been near the place for ten years! All I'm saying is that I'm *not* spoiled, I've worked hard to get where I am, and I don't intend to let the firm go bankrupt. There isn't even any danger of it—we're doing well and if we get that big Arabian order——'

'Which could have been even bigger if you'd only been a little more adventurous——'

'—if we get that big Arabian order,' Trina repeated a little louder, 'there'll be nothing at all to worry about——'

'For a few months, anyway.'

'*Ever!*' She stared at him helplessly. 'Look, I don't *know* why Dad insisted that you should be brought in, but it wasn't for any of the reasons you think. Maybe he just thought a woman M.D. wouldn't command as much respect outside—I don't know, there still are people who think that way—maybe he just wanted your name on the letterhead or something. But I'm sure it was no more than that. He never intended all this argument and upset. He couldn't have!'

'So why indulge in it? Why not just accept the situation and let's talk things over calmly? I still think we need to have a long discussion on policy.'

'But I'm *not* indulging in it! It's you——' Trina stopped suddenly, aware that her voice had risen shrilly and that there were more people coming along the track, giving them curious glances. Griff grinned suddenly and she glowered at him. There was nothing she'd have liked better at that point than to hit him, good and hard, but she could hardly do that here on the Edge, on a Sunday in full view of half a dozen sightseers. That wasn't the sight they'd come to see, though no doubt they'd find it equally interesting! Controlling her impulse with some difficulty, she turned away, hoping that her stiff back expressed dignity, and walked on along the track.

Griff fell in beside her again and she muttered: 'Why don't you just go away? I came up here for some peace and quiet, to relax. That just doesn't seem possible with you around.'

'Oh, but it is,' he said cheerfully. 'You'd be surprised how relaxed I can be, in certain circumstances.' She shot him a suspicious glance but his expression was blandly innocent. 'Besides, I'm afraid I have to walk back with you. My car's at your house. I came over to invite you out for a meal this evening and Mrs Aston told me you'd come up here.'

Trina felt trapped. Not only did she have to finish her walk with him, but she wouldn't even be able to get rid of him when she arrived home. No doubt he would expect to be invited in for tea—and although Trina herself would have ignored the idea, Mrs Aston wouldn't. She was probably baking scones and a Victoria sponge at this very minute.

'Well?' Griff enquired after a few minutes. 'Will you come out with me this evening?'

'I don't really see any point, do you? We'd only argue.'

'But we don't have to,' he said persuasively. 'We never used to. I always had the idea that you rather liked me, in fact. Oh, I realised that it was nothing more than a schoolgirl crush—rather sweet, the way you used to hang around the glasshouse watching me—but you must admit we had some quite interesting conversations.'

Trina felt herself blush scarlet. Was there nothing this man missed? She'd hoped since that he'd never realised why she hung around the chair of which he was leading workman. At least he might have forgotten it—or never mentioned it. But that wasn't Griff's way, she thought bitterly. Give him a weapon, some means of putting her down, and he'd use it.

'As you say, that was just a silly teenage infatuation,' she said coldly. 'It didn't last. I suppose everyone goes through these experiences when they're too young to know better.'

'Oh, of course,' he agreed smoothly. 'We won't even bother to mention it again. So you'll come?'

'I didn't say that. I still don't see the point.'

'The point is, to try to get to know each other properly so that we *don't* have these arguments,' he explained. 'Don't you think that makes sense? We'll just pretend we're no more than friends—acquaintances, if you'd rather. Chat about this and that. Find out what we have in common——'

'I can tell you that—nothing!'

'But you see, you don't really know that, do you? Look, you might just as well come. I don't suppose you've anything else planned or you'd have said so. No sense in our both spending the evening alone.'

'Well, you don't need to,' Trina told him. She glanced up at his face, her heart racing suddenly, and added in a queer, strangled voice: 'Why don't you take Julia?'

There was a long silence. Griff's face closed and Trina felt a twinge of alarm. What had she said to make him look like that? He knew that she'd met Julia, knew what she must believe was the relationship between them. So why should he look like that—like a thunderstorm about to unleash all its fury?

A quiver of fear shook Trina, but there was nothing she could do about it. She walked in silence, afraid to say more, her mind teeming with questions she dared not ask.

Just what *was* Julia Meredith to Griff Tyzak? And why should he react like that at the mere mention of her name?

CHAPTER FIVE

THE fine weather didn't last long and it was cold and sleety again during the next week. Trina made the journey into Stourbridge each day along treacherously icy roads, wrapped in her warmest clothes—layers of thick sweaters and scarves in the bright colours that she loved and had always given her confidence. Except, she thought ruefully, when faced with elegance in the person of Julia Meredith.

Griff had not answered her question about Julia as they walked back from the Edge on Sunday, and they had arrived back at Compson House in a strained silence. More because she knew Mrs Aston would expect it than for any other reason, Trina issued her stiff invitation to tea, which Griff refused with equally distant politeness. Nothing more was said about his own invitation to dinner.

Trina watched him drive away in the dark green Volvo, then turned to go indoors feeling strangely empty. The day hadn't been the success it had promised to be. The sky had darkened now and the sun was low behind heavy grey clouds; a raw wind had sprung up and as Trina stood there she felt a spike of cold on her cheek as something began to fall—snow, perhaps or ice-cold rain. Shivering, she opened the front door and stepped into the warmth of the hall.

'Mr Tyzak not coming in?' Mrs Aston enquired, appearing from the kitchen. 'I've got tea ready, thought you could have it by the fire.'

'No, he had to go.' Trina stripped off her jacket and boots. 'I'll have tea, though, Mrs Aston. Don't you bother—I'll come and fetch it. I'm looking forward to that fire, I must say. And a nice hot bath when I've thawed out a bit.'

Mrs Aston hovered around her as she collected a tray

from the kitchen, piling her plate with fresh scones and a couple of crumpets to toast over the fire. 'He's a nice man, that Mr Tyzak,' she chatted. 'Always did think so, and he hasn't spoiled with the years. Nice to see him around here again. Your father was always fond of him, I remember.'

'I suppose he must have been. I don't really know why.' Trina lifted the tray, then remembered the toasting-fork and rummaged for it in a drawer.

'Oh yes. Looked on him almost as a son, I sometimes thought. Well, you must know that yourself. He's a big help at the works, I'm sure.' Mrs Aston paused thoughtfully. 'Strange he never married.'

'Perhaps he's impossible to live with,' Trina suggested, thinking that this was probably true, but Mrs Aston snorted disbelievingly.

'Never! No more than any other man, anyway. No, I reckon he just hasn't found the right young lady yet. He will—and she'll be a lucky girl, mark my words.' She gave Trina a speculative glance. 'A very lucky girl.'

Trina escaped with her tray, feeling shaken. Was *that* the way minds were working—or was it just Mrs Aston putting two and two together to make a whole lot more! My God, she thought, closing the library door behind her, does everybody think the same? That Dad brought Griff in as a prospective husband for me—and, in due course, sole Managing Director, with me at home looking after the family?

Well, that was something that certainly wasn't going to happen! And it was something that she could quite easily prove wrong—and would. It would take only a short time before anyone was quite definitely disillusioned about any idea that she and Griff were anything else but reluctant partners. Thank goodness she hadn't gone out with Griff tonight! And any other suggestions of meeting socially would have to be very firmly squashed.

Her campaign began next morning when Griff came breezing into her office, big and bulky in his sheepskin jacket, and clapped Trina's shoulder jovially, his eyes already on the mail. He seemed to have forgotten already about yesterday, and Trina stepped hastily away from him, blushing as she caught Jean's eye on them. Her voice was as cold as the morning as she returned his greeting and pointed out that she had already divided the letters into two piles as arranged.

'Mm, so I see.' He shrugged out of his jacket and smiled at Jean. 'Any coffee going, Jean? It's raw this morning. Not like yesterday, hm, Trina?'

Trina decided not to answer this. She sat down at her desk and began to open letters, putting them in a neat pile beside her to be read when the envelopes had been disposed of. Nothing very outstanding—and then she stopped with a gasp of pleasure.

'What is it?' Griff was opposite her, going through his pile. Trina looked up with sparkling eyes.

'The Arabian order—it looks as if we're going to get it! It's not a firm commitment, but it seems pretty definite. Just one or two last queries to be settled, and then we can start. Isn't that marvellous?'

'Let's see.' Griff took the letter and read it. 'Mm, not bad at all. Not a firm order, as you say, but it certainly looks hopeful. What exactly does it involve—what pieces do they want?'

'Oh—glasses, not for wine, of course, but they want a kind of goblet for fruit juices and sherbets—jugs for the same—bowls in various sizes for fruit and desserts, confort dishes, vases—platters. Quite a variety. We shall need to get the whole glasshouse on it once we do start.'

'So we'd better step up production of our normal lines in the meantime.' Griff stood up. 'I'll talk to Nicklin right away. By the way, what's the design for the Arabian stuff? I haven't seen it yet.'

Trina took a glass from the array that stood around her windowsill. 'This is it.' She'd already forgotten her antagonism in the excitement of receiving the letter, and she bent her head close to his to show him the design. 'It's very elaborate—we'll have to get the cutters on overtime! You see, a very complex pattern of straight cuts with the falcon and this rather pretty flower in intaglio on lozenges on each side. The flower is apparently quite important to the Sheikh's family too. He sent some specimens by air for me to copy, and some drawings. It's a desert flower of some kind, only blooms when there's been rain, which isn't very often.'

'Mm.' Griff turned the glass this way and that so that the light glanced off it. 'Yes, very nice. Not an easy design, though. Are all the pieces the same?'

'Some of the larger pieces have a different design—at least, it's the same basically, but there's more intaglio, or copper-wheel engraving. There's one very large bowl which will have an engraving of the Sheikh's palace and gardens all round it. Derek will do that, of course.'

'And you did the designs?'

'Most of them. We had a lot of discussions, of course.'

Trina waited hopefully. But Griff said no more, merely grunted again and then sat down to go on with the post. 'I'll see Nicklin when I've done this. You and Jean can cope with most of it, I should think.'

Trina felt her temper begin to rise. 'Oh, can we? And what do you propose to do while we're—coping?'

Griff gave her a surprised glance. 'Why, get on with organising the works for this order, of course. See what other orders we've got, do a bit of time-estimating— make up a progress-chart so that we can see the situation at a glance. Make sure we can fulfil all our commitments—no sense in losing established customers for a one-off job, however lucrative it might be. Oh, and while I'm doing that could you get out the files on that——'

Trina interrupted him. Her eyes blazed with anger as she faced him across the desk, and Jean, coming in with the coffee, stood unnoticed in the doorway, staring in astonishment before hastily backing out again.

'Just you get this straight, Griff Tyzak,' Trina began through clenched teeth. 'I'm not, repeat *not* your secretary, dogsbody, Girl Friday or even personal assistant. I'm Joint Managing Director of a glassworks *my great-grandfather* founded and which has been in my family ever since. I have equal responsibility with you, hell take it, and I make no secret of the fact that I neither like the situation nor understand it—but as long as it holds, I am *not* going to be relegated to second place and left kicking my heels, dealing with routine letters and *getting out files* while *you* strut round *my* factory and make all the arrangements for an important order!' Her voice rose steadily as she continued and Griff made a slow flapping motion with one hand, directing her to lower it. 'And I will *not* be quiet, either!' she shouted at him. 'Just stop patronising me—stop treating me like a child—and remember who I am! If this mail needs a Managing Director to deal with it, we'll deal with it together, all right? And we'll do all those other things together too. I am *not* going to be pushed out, Griff, by you or anybody else, and you'd better get that quite clear!'

There was a long silence. Shakily, Trina sat down again. She wanted, for some absurd reason, to cry, but she kept her eyes fixed firmly on him. They just had to get this straight.

'Finished?' Griff enquired at last, mildly.

Trina nodded. 'So long as you take notice of what I say. I've told you, Griff, I won't——'

He held up his hand. 'Okay, okay, don't let's have an action replay. I'll say one thing for you, Trina, you certainly know how to get going. Yes, you've made yourself quite clear—and not only to me. Most of the office must have heard that little diatribe! Just when I thought we might be getting them to believe in some kind of harmony between us, too.'

'And that's another thing,' Trina began, remembering Mrs Aston's remarks, but Griff held up both hands as if to ward off another attack.

'Not another outburst, Trina, please,' he begged. 'I couldn't stand it. And whatever you were going to say, I'm sure it can wait until we've got these orders sorted out. Now—we'll carry on with the post together, shall we? And then we'll *both* talk to Robert Nicklin and see how the works is placed before we *both* draw up our *joint* progress-chart. Does that suit you?'

Trina nodded. She had an uneasy feeling that he was laughing at her, but as long as she got her way in this she didn't care too much about that. She had made up her mind that Griff was going to accept her as his equal—and doing the filing and replying to letters wasn't going to achieve that. A stand had to be made.

'Where's that coffee?' Griff asked a moment or two later. 'With the amount of work we've got to get through, we're going to need plenty of stimulation!'

It was several days before Trina was able to make another of her tours of the glassworks, and she was pleased that the chance had occurred when Griff was out of the way. He had to see the owner of his cottage about various matters, he had told her, and Thursday morning was the only time possible. He should be in after lunch, however, and nothing too urgent should crop up before then.

'Nothing that I can't deal with, anyway,' Trina said sweetly. She and Griff had been very correct with each other since their confrontation on Monday, and the politeness was beginning to get her down. She supposed it was better than the energy-draining arguments, but it seemed very unreal and the thought of a morning without Griff was as good as a holiday.

Having dealt quickly with the post, she set off down the rabbit-warren of passages and corridors for the glasshouse. Most glass factories were built on much the same lines, she had found, and there seemed to be two main reasons for it: one, that the vast areas needed by the glasshouse and the cutting-shops made a spreading design inevitable, and two, that the Victorians, who were responsible for many of the factories, just liked building that way. There was plenty of space in those days, so why not use it? Big was prosperous, and so on.

The warmth and clatter of the glasshouse hit her, as usual, the moment she opened the door. She paused as she always did to enjoy the sight of the men moving rhythmically around the domed furnace with their long irons, gathering the red-hot glass and passing it to each other with a precision of timing that came from long practice. She wondered if they had done any singing lately; one of the delights of her life had been when one man would start a song, his deep voice made all the more powerful by the development of lungs and chest muscles that were more usually used for glassblowing. He would sing only a few words before the others would join in, some at once, others more gradually, until eventually the entire glasshouse boomed and resonated with the sound of their voices. People talked about miners singing as they left the pits, Trina had sometimes thought, but no one ever mentioned the choirs of the glasshouses. It was a private joy.

But there had been no singing in recent weeks. It was understandable after her father's death, but she was hoping that the old atmosphere would have returned by now. It would be a pity if the habit died.

The men glanced up and nodded at her as she went by, but she was disturbed to notice a slight restraint in their manner. It was so faint that she wondered if she were imagining it; but when even Trevor, usually so vociferous, merely grunted a 'good morning', she began to be seriously worried.

'What's the matter, Trevor?' she asked. 'Still worried about your daughter?'

'Oh, she's all right,' he answered. 'It's nothing but weddings in our house now. Who's to be bridesmaids, what they're to wear, what flowers she'll carry—seems there's no end to it. And do I get a say in it? You have to be joking! Just the poor mug who pays for it all, that's me. Well, I suppose that's what I'm here for. You'd think they got cheaper to run as they got older, daughters, but they don't.'

'She'll be off your hands then, though,' Trina said, trying to reassure him, but he didn't seem to find much comfort in the idea, and, muttering something about it being grandchildren next, he went back to his work.

Trina continued thoughtfully on her tour. Trevor's grumbles had been, as always, complaints made to hide his real feelings of pride and delight in his pretty daughter, who had been Carnival Queen last year. But Trina had sensed that they were also hiding something else; another dissatisfaction that he hadn't wanted to discuss with her. And it wasn't something personal, she was sure. Some of the other men had given her the same impression—a kind of wariness in their faces and voices, a withdrawal of the kindly affection they usually showed her.

Was it because she was now Managing Director? Or was there some other reason?

She stopped by Derek's bench and watched him for a while. He was working on a special order today, a set of goblets for a silver wedding anniversary, and whoever was going to receive them ought to be very pleased, Trina thought as she picked one up to look at it. She hadn't designed it herself, but she'd seen it in design stage and thought there was an idea there that might be expanded for her 'Seasons' range. The garland of spring flowers would fit in very well with that. She made a note to bring it up for discussion later.

'Everything all right, Derek?' she enquired casually. 'Haven't seen you much this week.' She always seemed to be saying that to him—must watch it, or they'd be getting talked about! Although—an idea struck her and she stopped in her tracks—that might not be such a bad thing. It would scotch any rumours about her and Griff? And show that young Lothario that every woman he met *wasn't* just waiting to fall into his arms.

'Why don't you come up to Compson House for supper one evening?' she invited him. 'We could have a really long talk. I wasn't very good company the other evening, I know. Will you come, so that I can make it up to you?'

'Thanks, I'd like to.' Derek narrowed his eyes to examine his work. 'Which evening?'

'Tonight? Tomorrow?' He shook his head. 'What about Sunday, then?' He was very occupied all of a sudden—Trina wondered in some panic if he might have found himself another girl-friend. 'Sunday's all right? Come along about seven—earlier if you like. I'll cook you supper with my own fair hands and we'll be all cosy together.'

Derek nodded and picked up another goblet. Trina smiled at him and took the hint. Once he was busy with an interesting job, Derek's attention could only be partly distracted. She walked on through the whine of the cutting shop, stopped to admire various pieces of work, had a word with the girl working on the *biebuyck*, whose father worked in the acid-room and had been ill recently, and then made her way back to her own office.

'Oh, there you are, Trina,' said Jean, appearing from her own office. 'Robert Nicklin's here, wants to see you.'

'Oh, come in, Robert.' Trina pulled a chair out for him and then sat behind the desk. She watched with affection as he came in. Robert Nicklin had been a part of her life ever since she could remember. Short and stocky, he had started as an apprentice under her grandfather and risen to the position of Works Manager before becoming Works Director. He knew all the men well, had been an active member of the National Union of Flint Glass Workers, and could generally be relied upon to have his finger on the pulse of the whole factory. Little escaped him; Trina was aware that her father had found him invaluable and knew that she was going to do the same.

'I'm glad you came in,' she told him. 'I've been wanting a word with you.'

'And I've been wanting one with you.' Robert's Black Country accent was as strong as ever as he settled himself in the chair. 'Griff not here this morning?'

'No, he had some private business to attend to.' Was this why he'd come—because he wanted to speak to her alone? But Robert pursed his lips as if to say he might as well make the best of it, then, and began to make all his usual preperations to speak; fumbling for his pipe and tobacco, packing the brown shreds into the bowl, sucking thoughtfully and shifting about in his seat until Trina wanted to scream.

Instead, she decided to start first. 'I've just been round the foundry,' she remarked. 'There's an odd atmosphere, Robert—I couldn't quite make it out. As if the men wanted to say something but couldn't. What is it, do you know—or am I imagining it?'

Robert's small brown eyes darted at her face as she began to speak, then looked away again quickly. It was an almost exact reproduction of the wariness she had noticed in some of the men and she felt more than ever sure that something was wrong. But what? Was Robert going to tell her—or was he going to pretend all was well?

To her relief, he didn't. He sighed, smacked his lips once or twice in a habit he had, and scratched his chest. Now we'll hear it, she thought.

'You're not imagining it, Trina,' he said at last. 'The men are—well, they're a bit worried, see. They don't think they know what's going to happen—to the firm and everything, I mean. Everything seems a bit uncertain. I mean, we all know the firm's doing all right—but some of the other factories aren't, and it worries them a bit. Nobody wants to find themselves redundant.'

'But there's no question of that!' Trina protested, horrified. 'You must tell them Robert.'

'Well, I will. But I think it'd come better from you— or Griff.' Robert paused and Trina realised, with a sinking heart, that there was more to come. 'And that's the other thing, you see. This business of you both being in charge. It seemed a good idea—but people are beginning to say that you and he don't agree, and when that happens—well, you get a pull-devil, pull-baker situation that does nobody any good.'

'No, of course not.' Trina thought hard. Evidently news of arguments between her and Griff had got around—and it wasn't surprising after the way they'd yelled at each other in this very office. No wonder the

men had been cautious! They must have been feeling
that the whole firm could collapse around their ears at
any moment. Unless they were reassured—and
quickly—they'd begin to look for jobs in other
foundries. And with the Arabian order coming up,
together with the rush on normal orders that would
have to be arranged to make way for it, Compson
Crystal couldn't afford to lose anyone at all. Quite apart
from the fact that so many of the men had long family
connections with Compson's, and Trina could not bear
the idea of those connections being severed.

'All right, Robert,' she said. 'We'll arrange a meeting
as soon as possible, in the canteen, and we'll tell them
the correct position then. Don't worry about it.' And
for that meeting, she and Griff would—somehow—
have to present a united front. She just hoped that
wouldn't start any more rumours!

Trina was relieved to find that Griff was in total
agreement that a meeting should be held with the entire
workforce, and on Monday morning they both arrived
early so that it could be done before work started for
the day. It was still dark when Trina parked her car and
she shivered in the biting wind. Somehow, this was
proving to be a very long winter, and she yearned for
some sign of spring. Perhaps when the banks were
studded with primroses and hedges green with new
leaves she would feel better.

As it was, an uneasy depression seemed to be stealing
over her at odd moments, so that she found herself
staring unseeingly into space when she ought to be
working, or shivering in front of a fire that had long
gone out, without any real idea of how the time had
passed.

She still missed her father desperately and longed for
someone to turn to—someone who would be strong
enough to cope and understanding enough not to need
the explanations she could not give, even to herself.
She'd hoped that Derek might be the one, but although
he was obviously concerned for her, nothing he said

seemed to hit the right note, and she had been glad to see him go after their fireside supper last night. It was very depressing, she'd thought as she made her way to bed. There must be *someone*. But who—and where?

She walked across to the canteen with Griff. It was a separate building, used as a club as well, and she had often attended dances and social evenings there. The employees used it for private functions too—weddings and anniversaries had been celebrated here, as well as one or two fund-raising events when the local hospital had run an appeal.

Perhaps Trevor would have his daughter's reception here. Trina smiled to herself—he was obviously far prouder than he would admit of the pretty girl who was costing him so much. And Trina felt quite sure that he didn't really begrudge a penny of it.

They had agreed that Trina would speak to the men first, then Griff. Trina was surprised to find herself nervous—ridiculous, she told herself, when she knew all these people personally and had spoken to them hundreds of times. But *en masse*, in this more formal atmosphere, it was different, and she heard her voice shake a little as she began to speak, telling them that she was glad they had all come, that she knew how much her father had valued them and their work and that she knew she was going to feel the same loyalty towards them that she knew they felt towards her—or, rather, towards Compson Crystal. 'Many of us have ties with the firm that go back two or three generations,' she said. 'That counts for a lot with me, and I think it does with you too. I don't want to see any of those ties broken and I shall do my utmost to see that there's no danger of that happening. Compson's will go on, as before——' she felt Griff stiffen slightly at that, but she went on determinedly, '—and I think that within a few months any uncertainty you may have felt will have been completely dispelled.'

She sat down. That was as far as she dared go in hinting at the new order, since it wasn't yet final, but already the men were looking speculatively at each other, their faces lighting with interest and hope.

Griff stood up and the little buzz of conversation stopped. Trina watched their expressions, trying to divine their attitude towards him. Many of them knew him from his time in the factory, and she wondered how they felt about seeing him stand before them as Managing Director—*joint* Managing Director. Were they pleased that he had found such favour, or did they resent it?

But their attentiveness as he spoke seemed to indicate respect, if nothing else. And Trina had to give him her own, rather grudging, admiration as he skilfully introduced the subject of pay rises and broke news that was pleasant to nobody.

'You all know we're in the middle of a recession,' he told them. 'That's hitting everyone—even Compson Crystal. No, we're not going bankrupt—far from it— and I'm not announcing any redundancies. Nor do I think we shall have to in the foreseeable future. What I am announcing, however, is that there won't be any wage increases—again, in the foreseeable future.' There was a low murmur from the floor and Trina watched anxiously. She'd been worried about this move, even though long talks with Malcolm Jennings, the accountant, had convinced her it was necessary. 'We've thought long and hard about this,' Griff went on, 'and there really isn't any alternative—not if you're all to keep your jobs. And it's in our interests, as well as yours, that you do. There's not a man or woman among you that we can afford to lose.' That was good, Trina thought. And true. The entire factory worked as a team, just as each 'chair' of men in the glasshouse did. One key person missing could throw production completely.

'But it's not all bad news,' Griff continued. 'There's a chance of a large order in the near future, and to enable us to accept that we'll have to work fast on our normal orders. That means overtime, so your pay packets won't be too slim. I can't say any more about that now, it's not final, but there's a fighting chance. And if that doesn't come off—well, we've a few other ideas up our sleeves as well.' He paused and looked around the faces that were ranged in front of him. 'I consider it an honour to be back with you,' he said simply. 'Compson Crystal gave me my start and I owe it a great deal. Now's my chance to pay back that debt. You can rest assured that I shall—and that Trina Compson and I will work together to make sure that all our futures are secure.'

He sat down and the men burst into a storm of clapping. Trina watched them, a mist of tears before her eyes. Griff had made a good speech and they were now firmly on his side. He'd even included her with that hint at the end that all was well between them. She wished desperately that it could be true. It was clearly what the employees wanted; it was what her father had wanted; Griff had even said that was what *he* wanted. So why wasn't it working?

And if it still didn't work—what then? How long would she be able to tolerate the situation—the pain of seeing Griff each day, the way her heart thumped when she heard his voice, the weakness she still hadn't been able to overcome when he looked at her or touched her, even accidentally?

As the men filed out, Trina caught some of their conversation. It was plain that almost to a man they were wholeheartedly for Griff. Any grumbling about wages was minor and little more than routine. Nobody really resented the idea. They were all too anxious to keep their jobs and to keep the firm going.

Robert Nicklin leaned across and spoke to Griff.

'Well done, lad! That was just what they needed—a bit of straight talking and a hint of better times to come. I just hope the Sheikh comes across with that order now!'

'So do I,' said Griff, grinning. 'By the way, Trina, I won't be in tomorrow. Got to go to London.' He said no more, obviously not intending to explain why and, although Trina was immediately consumed with curiosity, she would not let herself ask. Probably to visit a girl-friend, she thought unreasonably. Julia Meredith, perhaps. She hadn't been seen around Stourbridge or Bridgnorth—at least, by Trina—since the night at the Swan, and she looked more like London than the Black Country.

Well, he was welcome to go. Trina looked forward to the times when Griff was absent from the works. Yet, oddly, when they came she never seemed able to settle properly. It was as if she was even more on edge when he was away then when he was there—if that were possible.

As it was still early, they went back to the office and Jean made coffee before the post arrived. There was nothing particularly exciting or important in it and it was soon dealt with. Neither of them had any appointments, either, and Trina leaned back in her chair, stretched luxuriously, and remarked that she would go and do some work on her 'Seasons' designs.

'Good idea,' Griff said absently. His eyes moved over Trina's slender figure, revealed in her clinging jersey as she stretched herself, and she hastily dropped her arms, feeling a blush spread like fire from her neck to her temples. The memory of his kisses in Holy Austin Rock came back to her in full force and she dropped her eyes from his face, aware from the glint in his eye that he was remembering them too. Once again she cursed herself for having allowed it to happen. How *could* she? She hadn't only submitted to his behaviour— she'd joined in, returning kiss for kiss, caress for caress. She could still feel the pressure of his lips on hers, the way his mouth had played with hers, the sensation as his probing fingers had found their way under her sweater to her bare skin. Even now the weakness threatened to invade her; if he touched her now there would be no hope and she had a dreadful feeling that he knew it. But he made no move; simply sat there, smiling slightly, until Trina wanted to throw something at him.

She got up abruptly and moved towards the door. That meant passing him, and she prayed that he wouldn't touch or try to prevent her. But he still didn't move, and Trina reached the door safely, hardly knowing whether to be relieved or disappointed. Once again she scolded herself for being so feeble. It wasn't even as if she loved him, for heaven's sake! It was a physical attraction, nothing more. Lust, if you want a less pleasant—and more truthful—word, she thought as she reached her own design office and leaned against the closed door as if she had gained sanctuary. Yes, lust. Not a very creditable characteristic—one of the seven deadly sins, in fact. Nothing to be proud of, that was certain. And the sooner she could get herself out of it, the better.

Trina worked steadily for the rest of the day. It was the first full day she'd had on designing for several weeks and she found herself relaxing in the work she loved, all her problems receding as she planned arrangements of ice crystals, snowflakes and frosted spiders' webs. There was a dozen different patterns to draw and she went through several permutations, trying the effect with intaglio and freehand work to see which would be most effective. Her desk was covered with sheets of paper when she discovered that lunchtime had come and gone, and it was beginning to grow dark again.

Suddenly aware of feeling tired, she yawned and rubbed her eyes. It was probably as well to stop for today anyway. The works would be finishing soon and if she slipped away now she would escape the rush of traffic along the roads.

She sorted out her drawings and left them tidy on her desk. Then she pulled her duffle coat around her, turned off the light, and went out to her car.

Griff's Volvo was parked next to it. So he hadn't left for London yet, though she'd heard him tell Robert Nicklin that he was going today. Trina shrugged and unlocked her door; it was none of her business where he went, or when.

As she ducked into the car, she glanced up and saw a movement in the door to the offices. An unfamiliar figure stood framed in the light for a moment—a figure wrapped close in a silver mink jacket, with a flame of hair spilling down over the thick, high collar.

Julia Meredith. As Trina watched, she stepped out of the door, followed by Griff. And with arms linked, they both made their way across the little car park.

In sudden panic, Trina switched on the ignition and reversed the car away, turning at the same time to face the road. She had to get away before they reached the Volvo. A friendly chat with Julia Meredith was something she just couldn't face!

CHAPTER SIX

THE weather worsened over the next few days and Trina began to hate the drive in from Compson House to the glassworks each morning. She was puzzled by this; she'd done the drive for several years now, sometimes with her father but frequently alone, and during that time there had been two particularly severe winters, with heavy snowfalls and thick ice on the country roads. Yet she had taken them in her stride and seldom been unable to reach the factory. So why should this winter's storms, more uncomfortable than severe, cause her such bother?

Perhaps because it was such indefinite weather, she thought, peering through the murk of the late afternoon as she made her way home. Snow was a nuisance, but it was exciting and beautiful. This was just plain ghastly—not really snow, certainly not rain, just cold, wet sleet that soaked into your very bones and turned each day into a kind of half-night, so that the lights could never be turned off and the sun was a thing of the past.

She felt very tired as she reached home and put the car away. Her depression seemed to have increased, though she had expected it to lessen with Griff's absence. But this time it hadn't worked; the office had seemed strangely empty without his vibrant presence and even the factory, where the men were once again greeting her with open faces and ready grins, seemed to have lost some of its excitement. The daily work that she would have shared with Griff became a chore and even her designs lacked vitality. If this went on, she thought, she would have to see Dr Mansfield. Perhaps she was run down, needed a tonic. Or some sunshine, though there was no possibility of a holiday just now. But the last time she had seen the sun had been that day on the Edge, when Griff had held her in his arms and

100

kissed her with a tenderness that it hurt to remember; although she kept on remembering it in spite of the pain, like probing an aching tooth just to see if the sensation were still there. . . .

She had changed into an old pale blue tracksuit, with legwarmers, and a thick, soft woollen shawl round her shoulders, and was lying on the couch in the sitting-room trying to concentrate on a magazine when she heard the sound of the doorbell. Trina groaned. Whoever it was, she didn't feel like seeing them. Perhaps it was someone for Mrs Aston and they'd mistaken the door. . . . But as she swung her feet to the carpet, she heard voices in the hall. Mrs Aston's—and someone elses. Someone whose deep, velvety tones made her heart suddenly race, caught her breath in her throat and brought a treacherous weakness to her limbs, so that she dared not stand up but stayed there, half lying among the cushions, watching the door with wide, half frightened eyes.

As usual, Griff Tyzak seemed to bring a scent of a different world into the room with him—a world of energy and dynamism, where tiredness and depression were unknown and incisive vitality and vigour were the norm. He was already half out of his sheepskin coat as he came through the door, his eyes alight, and he came straight over to Trina and threw his jacket on to a chair before standing to gaze down at her with triumph glowing in his face.

'Griff?' Trina said faintly. 'I—I wasn't expecting you tonight.' She moved, meaning to take up a more formal position, but before she could do so Griff was sitting on the edge of the couch, far too close for comfort, and instinctively she shrank back against the cushions, wondering rather frantically whether Mrs Aston were within call.

'I know you weren't expecting me,' he answered cheerfully. 'But that doesn't matter, does it? I've got some news for you, Trina—good news!' His face was more elated than she had ever seen it, and he seemed to have shed ten years, becoming again the young Adonis she had worshipped in the glasshouse. A picture of him then, stripped to the waist and swinging the heavy iron as if it were a straw in the wind, punched into Trina's mind, and she shook with a tremor she couldn't control. Griff smiled and moved closer. He radiated excitement and delight and she wondered what his news could be. Something to do with Julia? But why come and tell her?

'The order,' he was saying, and she jerked into attention. 'The Arabian order—we've got it, Trina! All signed, sealed—and waiting for delivery. And there's nothing to stop us making a start on it straightaway— none of our other orders are urgent, and we can be putting some of them through at the same time. But the main thing is, we can make a start. How's that? Isn't it terrific news?'

Trina's eyes widened and she heard herself give a little gasp. 'The Arabian order—*confirmed*?' she exclaimed. 'But when? How do you know? There was no news in the office today. What's happened?'

'*I've* happened,' Griff grinned. 'All right, so I'm gloating—but wouldn't you? Don't I have a right? And wasn't it worth a couple of days in the big city? Well, Trina, what do you say?'

'The big—you mean London? Is *that* why you went? But that could have been disaster—you could have fouled up the whole thing! It's taken us months of negotiation and you go bulldozing in like a—a——'

'Bull in a glasshouse,' Griff finished helpfully. 'But it *wasn't* a disaster, was it? In fact, it might well have been a disaster if I *hadn't* gone. They were trying to decide between us and Cadnam Glass. It could have as easily gone to them as to us.'

'So why—how did you persuade them?' Trina was still dazed by the news.

Griff tried unsuccessfully to look modest. 'My own personal charm, sales ability and persuasiveness,' he offered. 'Plus the fact that I happen to know one of the Sheikh's sons.'

'You do? But you never said!'

'I wasn't absolutely sure. I met him a few years ago—he bought a couple of pieces of my glass from a Bond Street shop and then came to see me. I had to go, to make certain he *was* the man I remembered—every Tom, Dick and Harry's called Mohammed out there, you know—and once I knew I was right—well, it was all plain sailing.'

'The old boys' network, in fact,' said Trina, unable to keep a note of sourness out of her voice. It hadn't been her designs that had swung the balance at all.

Griff gave her a sharp look. 'Not at all. I told you, they were having some difficulty in deciding—the only way I made any difference was that he'd met me before and knew the order would be met in time. And he liked my work, too, I suppose.'

'But those designs *weren't* your work—they were *mine*!' Was he going to take credit for *everything*? She glowered at him and, to her annoyance, he burst out laughing.

'Trina, don't be so touchy! He *knows* they were your designs. Don't worry, the order got through on its merits all right. I merely tipped the balance, that's all. Can you honestly say you're not pleased?'

Trina was caught. She wanted to say yes—but she knew she couldn't. Of *course* she was pleased. It meant security for the glassworks, for the men and their families, for herself. It meant that months of hard work had paid off. It could mean the opening up of a new market, with further orders to come.

'Yes, I'm pleased, of course I am,' she said, capitulating. And once she'd admitted that, everything else seemed easy. She smiled at Griff and asked: 'Would you like a cup of coffee—to celebrate?'

'I've got something better than that. It didn't need much chilling, in this weather, but I gave it to Mrs Aston as soon as I came in, to put in the fridge. She could be just about ready to bring it in now.' He sprang up from the couch and made for the door. 'Mrs Aston? Ah, there you are. Yes, we'll have it now—and bring a glass for yourself too. This is a very special occasion!'

The housekeeper bustled in, bearing a tray on which stood a bottle of champagne and three glasses—tall, slender flutes in Trina's favourite design. She beamed at them both and set the tray down, standing back to let Griff open the bottle.

'This is good news, I'm sure,' she began, taking her glass of sparkling liquid from Griff. 'I had a feeling, I must say—but with Miss Trina being so low lately I'd begun to worry something had gone wrong. But there, the path of true love never did run smooth, they say, and you both look happy enough now. Wouldn't your father have been pleased, miss, and your——'

'*Mrs Aston!*' Struggling between dismay, amusement and acute embarrassment, Trina managed at last to stop the flow of words. 'Mrs Aston, what are you talking about? Mr Tyzak and I are celebrating a big new order for the glassworks, that's all! What did you think——' She stopped. It was all too plain what Mrs Aston had thought, and the housekeeper's face was now what she herself would have called 'a picture' as she turned from one to the other, bemused and perturbed. And, touchingly, disappointed.

Trina hastened to reassure her. 'It's all right, Mrs Aston. Griff ought to have explained. It was a natural mistake—I—mean——' She caught Griff's sardonic eye and floundered '—well, anyway, drink your champagne. Let's have a toast to—to the Sheikh and his son. May there be many more weddings in the family—the Sheikh's family, I mean,' she finished in confusion.

Mrs Aston made her escape soon after that, obviously still somewhat upset about her *gaffe*, and Griff drew Trina down on the couch beside him. He filled their glasses again and held them together.

'Another toast,' he said quietly. 'To co-operation. What do you say, Trina?'

Trina reached out for her glass, but he kept his fingers on the stem so that she was compelled to respond. And anyway, was it such a bad idea? It was what her father had intended—what she herself had wanted, surely? And Griff had managed to finalise the order.

'Co-operation,' she agreed, and he let her have her glass.

They sat in companionable silence for a few moments. Trina watched the firelight striking jewel colours off the cut-glass in her hand. This was really what it was all about, wasn't it? The beauty and grace of crystal, enhancing homes, bringing sparkle to parties and radiance to tables; adding to the visual delight of any drink; making life just that little bit more worth living with exquisite shape and pattern, enduring even when other pleasures had dimmed.

So wasn't it foolish to quarrel over its making? Shouldn't it be the product of harmony and accord rather than conflict and hostility?

She was very much aware of Griff, sitting close beside her on the couch. The warmth of his body touched her skin through the loose tracksuit, and she could feel the slight movement of his breathing. Her heart began to beat in a slow, heavy rhythm that was somehow more intoxicating than the racing she had experienced at other times. Her skin tingled where Griff pressed lightly against her, and she shifted half-consciously to increase the pressure. The weakness she had so resented, while only dimly understanding it, began to steal over her body again, and her glass chattered against her lips as she took a sip of champagne.

Griff turned at the tiny sound. His eyes, the colour of autumn leaves, looked gravely into hers. Then he took the almost empty glass from Trina's nerveless fingers and set it gently on a small table at his side.

Trina could not speak as he turned back to take her in his arms, and as his lips touched hers, so softly and tenderly at first that she was barely aware of them and knew only a sudden flash of desire that shot through her body like an exploding firework, she realised that this was what she had been yearning for. It was this that had kept her awake at night, caused her to sit blankly over a cold fireplace, taken her mind off the designing that had once absorbed her. When she had cursed the weather it was because she longed, unknowingly, for Griff's kisses; when she roamed the house, lost and lonely, it was because she needed to be in his arms.

She had tried to reject the knowledge, refused to admit it—called it lust. But it was more than that; suddenly, blindingly, she knew that it was far, far more than that. And she sighed and gave herself up to his kisses, returning them as the passion mounted in her, knowing at last that it was love she felt for Griff Tyzak. Not the calf-love she had experienced as a schoolgirl, ten years ago; not the childish adulation she had felt even before that; but true adult love, raw and powerful, demanding satisfaction, insisting on fulfilment.

'Griff?' she murmured on a questioning note, and he gathered her more closely into his arms. A feeling of safety flooded over her—spiced with the danger of knowing that here was a man who had known a number of women, women as experienced as he. She trembled as his fingers pulled down the zip of her tracksuit top and his hand closed over the rounded breasts that were already taut with desire, stroking and massaging until she heard herself whimpering with pleasure and thrust herself hard against him, wanting to feel him closer, wanting to have nothing between them but the firelight.

Griff eased the tracksuit jacket back from her shoulders and she lay in his arms, bare shoulders shivering a little as he stormed kisses in the hollow of her throat, down her arms, lingering over the inner curve of her elbows and nipping the ends of her fingers, and then to her body, exploring the roundness of her breasts with lips and hands. Trina found her own hands moving of their own volition, tangling in his hair, tugging gently at his ears, trembling their way down his face so that he turned and planted a kiss in each of her palms. Somehow, she found, they were lying on the couch, and she let her legs move with his, twining and tangling, hard muscles throbbing against soft flesh, and the fire in his lips spread through her body, making her ache with longing, making her heart race so that she felt it would burst.

'Trina,' Griff muttered, his mouth against her breast. 'Trina, this is crazy—insane. We've got to talk, Trina—we've got to sort things out——'

'Don't,' she begged him. 'Don't let's say a word. Things go wrong when we talk, and I don't want them to go wrong any more. I love you, Griff—oh, I love you so much!'

There was an instant of startled silence. Trina heard her own words with a kind of astonishment—she'd never meant to say them, had scarcely begun to formulate them in her own mind, but she knew now, with absolute certainty, that they were true, and she drew him close again, eager to give him proof. But Griff took her wrists in his hands and, firmly but gently, removed them from around his neck. He raised himself above her and looked down into her eyes, his own almost black now as the pupils dilated.

'*What* did you say, Trina?' he breathed.

'I said, I love you.' She felt a calm assurance as she looked back at him, and she smiled with contentment. 'I suppose I always have. Only I've been fighting it, you see. Until——' her face crumpled suddenly as she felt again the despairing loneliness of the past few days '—until now. Oh, Griff, I've missed you so much!'

'And I've missed you, Trina,' he muttered, burying his face in her silvery hair. 'My God, but I've missed you!'

Joyfully triumphant, she met his lips again, without restraint, while her fingers busied themselves in unbuttoning his shirt so that she could feel the delicious sensation of skin against skin, her breasts teased by the friction of his hair-covered chest. She felt his heart beating strongly against her own, felt her blood sing as it pulsed around her body. The world outside had ceased to exist and there was nothing but this warm, firelit room, this wide, soft couch where two bodies merged in an increasing need to become one, to unite in a last burning effort to deny all differences, to justify their entire existence and to prove incontrovertibly the reason why they lived at all.

Griff's body stretched out alongside hers and she hugged him to her, feeling a strange completeness, as if she had only half existed until now, as if both physically and mentally she had never yet attained full growth. It was like being given a second arm after living a lifetime with only one—bewildering at first, yet with a glimpse already of joys to come.

Slowly, as if embarking on a voyage of discovery, she explored his body with her own, letting her hands make tentative forays, her mouth seek its own delights. This was indeed what she had wanted for so long, this was what she had missed, hardly knowing that she was missing anything, yet restless and frustrated. In Griff's powerful arms she could, she knew now, find complete fulfilment, a haven for all her unsatisfied passion, a source of new energy and happiness. And in a sudden eagerness, she pressed her body against his, whimpering for the response that would set her on fire and bring the release that only he could give her.

'Steady, darling, steady!' Griff held her close, his hands stroking her hair with a motion that was more soothing than passionate. 'Quieten down, my sweet. Let's not rush our fences.' He ran his hand lightly down from her hair to her breast and held it gently, as if it were fragile. 'Trina, look at me. Look at me and tell me I'm not dreaming.'

Trina opened eyes that were green as emeralds in the firelight. His own were as soft as a dove's wing, all steeliness gone, and her heart kicked as she recognised the feeling behind them. Almost involuntarily, his head come down to hers and the kiss they shared was of total accord.

'You're not dreaming,' she breathed against his lips, her fingers on his cheek. 'Or if you are, I am too. . . . Griff, I've been so lonely these past few weeks. Everything's gone wrong—I can't seem to find my place any more——'

'No?' He drew her hand down his body, and she gasped. 'Trina, you know damned well where your place is, and so do I. But—let's not rush things, hm? You talked about love, and that's serious. It's something I haven't come across much before.'

Trina's brows came together in a tiny frown. 'Griff?'

'Not the kind of love you're talking about,' he told her. 'And I have a feeling that you mean something pretty deep. Something that's not to be taken lightly— not to be rushed.' He smiled as he brushed the tousled hair back from her forehead. 'Let's go slowly, my darling. I don't want anything to be spoiled. I want you—I want us both—to enjoy all the little stops along the way. Isn't there a song that says much the same thing?'

Trina's mouth quivered with laughter. 'There is, but I wouldn't have thought you'd know it.'

'And why not?' he demanded sternly. 'Because it's a romantic song? And don't you think—even now—that I'm a romantic?' As she hesitated, he moved closer again and his lips just brushed hers as he whispered: 'Then that just proves what I'm saying, Trina. I want an old-fashioned, romantic courtship where you're concerned. The whole scene—roses, moonlight, candle-lit dinners, whatever turns you on. Is that quite—' he gave her a tiny kiss, punctuating his words with more until Trina was almost frantic with longing '— quite—clear?'

She could hardly form the words, but she knew he had to have an answer, and she nodded weakly and murmured, on a breath, 'It's quite clear, Griff—but I don't know—oh, Griff——'

'You don't know what?' He let his lips stray down to her breasts again, teasing the nipple with his teeth. 'What don't you know, Trina, my love?'

'I don't know if I can wait,' she managed, and her body arched towards him as if in involuntary confirmation.

'Then in that case——' Griff shifted away from her slightly and drew her tracksuit jacket over her to conceal the rosy breasts from his own gaze '—in that case we'd better call a halt now.' He sat up and lifted her towards him, looking seriously into her eyes. 'I mean it, Trina. I've had my own experiences, and believe me, it would be all to easy for me to take you now and I can tell you you'd enjoy it too. But it wouldn't be fair. Once that's happened, there's no going back—and, when it's for the first time, the build-up can be so delicious. I wouldn't want to deprive you of one second of that. We've got all the rest of our lives before us, Trina. Let's give ourselves something to remember.'

Slowly, Trina's racing blood calmed and she found herself curled in his arms, a curious peace stealing over her as they watched the firelight and talked in soft voices. What they talked about, she could never afterwards remember—perhaps it was of no importance, perhaps it was nonsense—but she knew at last that Griff was right, that however clamorous the body might be it was better to leave it not quite satisfied—until the right moment came. And before that moment she and Griff needed to know each other in other ways too; to explore this new relationship, to resolve the other conflicts between them.

At last Griff stirred and said he must go. The temperature had dropped this evening, he said, and there was more than a hint of snow in the air. And they both needed to be at the glassworks early next morning; now that the Arabian order had been definitely confirmed, there was a great deal to be organised if production were to begin as soon as possible.

He drew Trina to her feet and they stood in each other's arms, hearts beating together, lips telling each other silently of love and longing. Then, as Trina's blood began to thunder once again, Griff put her gently away from him and shook his head slightly.

'That's all for now, my sweet,' he murmured. 'But there's plenty more to come. . . . Don't come out with me. It's too cold.'

'Just a moment,' said Trina, her hand on his arm.

'There's something I want to show you, before you go. It's in the library—it won't take long.'

Central heating had prevented the library from being cold, but without the leaping flames of a log fire it seemed dull and lifeless. Trina hesitated on the threshold, then took Griff's hand and led him in. She left him standing in the middle of the room while she went to the glass-fronted case where the Chalice was kept.

'Look,' she said, bringing it to the table. 'It's the most precious thing we own—the Compson Chalice. Isn't it beautiful?'

Slowly Griff came forward and stood looking down at the great goblet, its heavy dark blue glass glowing faintly under the electric light. The colour showed dimly through the white of the enamel decoration; other parts were totally opaque, milk-white horses carved so delicately that the rippling of their muscles and the straining of their bodies seemed almost alive.

Trina watched as Griff put out both hands and lifted the vessel, turning it this way and that to examine its perfection. There was an odd, unfathomable expression on his face; he seemed strangely moved and she was glad that she had shown it to him.

'Is this the piece that was made in the early 1880's, just after Joshua Compson took over the factory?' he asked at last, his voice hushed.

'Yes, that's right.' Trina was surprised that he knew about it. 'I suppose Dad told you some time. It's lovely, isn't it?'

'Do you know who made it?'

'No—he was a man Joshua employed here, but I don't know any more than that. He doesn't seem to have made any more. Perhaps he left——' she stumbled over the words, not wanting Griff to take them as an implied reproach to himself. 'Perhaps he did other pieces and they were sold, but I've never seen the early records. I suppose it would be possible to find out.'

'Oh, almost certainly,' he said absently. Then he set the Chalice down again and looked at it for a few more moments before turning to her. 'Maybe we'll find out one day. But just now there are a lot of other things to think about. This will keep—don't you agree? I'm glad you showed it to me, though. You're right—it's beautiful. And very precious.'

'I think so,' Trina said softly, and they both gave it a final glance before she took it back to its case.

At the door, Griff took her in his arms, but he didn't draw her close. He stood looking down at her, his eyes shadowed, and Trina trembled a little at his expression. He'd said he wanted to wait, to take things slowly—but she wondered if he could. There was so much restrained passion in him, she could sense it in his arms, his fingertips, the hardness of his body. Wasn't there a danger that it might break loose without warning?

'We've got a lot of talking to do some time, Trina,' he said quietly. 'About the factory—and about ourselves. There are things I have to tell you about myself——'

'No,' she said quickly, laying her fingertips on his lips. 'I don't want to know, Griff. No confessions. Let's start from where we are tonight.'

He hesitated for a moment, then shrugged slightly.

'Very well. We'll leave it at that—for now, anyway. And this time I really am going.' He bent his head and gave Trina a kiss that was more warming than a thousand log fires. 'See you in the morning, my pet. And by God, I was right—it *is* snowing!'

Trina looked out after him. The snow was falling softly and steadily, already whitening the fields and blurring the outlines of the trees with a soft, clinging fleece. The thin covering on the drive glittered in the light that spilled from the door, and she thought ruefully that if it went on all night it could be several inches deep by morning.

Griff ducked his head out of his car window. 'Don't stand in the cold, Trina,' he called. 'And don't try to drive in tomorrow—I'll call for you. Goodnight!'

The Volvo purred away down the drive and Trina closed the door softly. Slowly she made her way back to the sitting-room and stood at the door for a moment, watching the dying glow of the fire and recreating the scene that had taken place there earlier.

Things changed so incredibly, she thought as she collected up the glasses and the empty bottle. When she had first entered this room this evening, she had been weighed down by a depression that she didn't even understand, tormented by a frustration she wouldn't acknowledge and irritated by longings she couldn't admit. Now it was all different. The world had been turned upside down and stood on its head, and everything had come right. It was like one of those puzzles, a transparent box of tiny balls that had to be jiggled about until all were in the correct position. As fast as you got one right another two fell out—but at last they had all fallen into place, and the puzzle was complete. Nothing could go wrong with it now.

Unless someone upset the box, she thought, and shivered suddenly. Don't be stupid, she scolded herself as she took the tray out to the kitchen and washed and dried the glasses carefully. What could go wrong now? She and Griff understood each other at last, and that was all that mattered. There would be no more misunderstandings.

Perhaps it wasn't really so surprising that Julia Meredith's face should come into her mind just then. But Trina pushed the vision firmly away. Griff had offered to tell her about Julia and she'd refused. It was all over—it had to be. Or why should he tell Trina that he loved her?

And he *had* told her that—hadn't he?

Next morning, as she had expected, Trina woke to a white world. Not that she had done much sleeping, she reflected as she drew the curtains aside and peered out. Her dreams had been too full of Griff to allow much rest. Several times she had woken convinced that she was lying in his arms, actually feeling their hardness about her, turning in them to offer him her lips and her love and only gradually realising that the sensations had been conjured up by a yearning heart. His kisses by the fire had burned her lips throughout the night, and the touch of his fingers on her breasts had been vividly real. There had been moments when she had wondered if it were all a dream, if it had actually happened. But when she came fully awake to the cold white reflection of snow on her bedroom ceiling, the warm contentment within her that contrasted so starkly with the icy world outside reassured her as to its truth.

The snow had stopped, but from the look of the sky there was more to come. The clouds lay like sullen lumps of lead so close to the ground that Trina felt she could almost touch them. As she watched, a gust of wind shook a flurry of snow from the branches of a silver birch and a few small birds flew across the garden looking for food.

Trina showered and dressed quickly, wrapping herself in warm trousers and a sweater of soft blue before scurrying downstairs to the warm kitchen. The big oil-fired Aga made sure it was always warm in there, and she gave a sympathetic glance at Misty, the cat, still tightly curled up in her basket. Misty seemed to know instinctively when the weather was bad outside and had been known to remain asleep in the warmth of the kitchen for almost a full twenty-four hours, rather than venture outside.

Comfortable, but dull, Trina thought as she made her porridge. She herself wouldn't want to forgo this delicious excitement, this lovely warmth, for anything. It made the whole of life look brighter, diminished difficulties, made everything worthwhile. And she wondered how she could ever have thought of marrying Derek. Derek was nice, dependable—and about as exciting as yesterday's tea. He would never have lit up the world for her like this, never have brought this sparkle to her life. And perhaps she couldn't have done it for him, either. They just weren't right for each other, friends though they might be. There would be some other girl for Derek, and she had a feeling that he knew it already.

There had been many women for Griff, she was sure of that. But this, he had intimated, was something different. This was love—and he hadn't 'come across' love before. So was he, too, looking out at the frozen world and thinking how different it looked this morning, and not just because of the snow? Was he too thinking that fairylights had been switched on and fireworks let off and the whole world turned around?

Almost as she wondered, the telephone shrilled and she jumped. She turned sharply and picked up the kitchen extension, her heart already racing, and when she heard the familiar, velvety tones she held the receiver to her with both hands, cradling it as if it were part of him.

'Trina? Is that you?' He waited only for her assent before going on. 'Trina, don't drive in this morning. I can't pick you up early—something's come up. But I'll fetch you around lunchtime, all right?'

Trina blinked. 'But why? What have you got to do?'

There was a slight pause before he said abruptly, 'Nevermind about that, Trina. Just do as I say, like a good girl, all right? I'll be along about twelve, right?'

A slow indignation began to burn in Trina's breast. 'No, it's not all right! There's a lot to be done, Griff, I can't take a morning off just because of a bit of snow. All right, so you can't come and pick me up—I never asked you to, as it happens. And I've driven in worse weather than this. I'll get myself in all right, you needn't worry.'

'I told you to do nothing of the kind——'

'And *I* told *you* I intend to. Don't patronise me, Griff, and don't bully me either. I'm quite capable of driving myself in and I shall do so. It's all the more important if you're not going to be there. How are we ever going to get this order met if we sit down and cry over a bit of snow?'

There was a short silence. Trina clutched at the receiver in dismay. Were they quarrelling already? And just because Griff was showing quite natural concern for her safety? She opened her mouth to apologise, to tell him she would wait after all, but Griff got in first.

'Do as I say, Trina,' he ordered harshly. 'I don't have time to waste arguing over the phone—we'll discuss it later, if you feel we must. But I'll be at Compson House at twelve noon and I expect you to be there—all right?' And the phone was banged down in her ear.

Trina gasped. So *that* was the way he thought he could treat her? Well, he would just have to learn differently, that was all! Start as you mean to go on, my girl, she thought determinedly as she went out into the hall and thrust her feet into warm fur-lined boots. No man was going to push *her* around, even if his name did happen to be Griff Tyzak. Love him she might—certainly did—but that didn't mean she was prepared to let him rule her. A partnership was what she had envisaged—not a Victorian marriage!

The phone rang again as she slammed the door behind her and went cautiously down the snow-covered steps, but Trina ignored it. If it was Griff, he could think what he liked—that she'd flouted his orders and left, or that she was merely sulking. In any case, she didn't feel like another argument right now.

Thank goodness, there was no ice under the snow, but Trina was well aware of just how treacherous freshly-fallen snow could be. Innocuous enough while you were keeping up a slow, steady speed, but touch the brakes and all hell could break loose. Fortunately her car had good tyres and she had handled it through the worst of last winter, so felt fairly confident as she backed it out of the garage. It would have been a good idea to have asked Mrs Aston to come out and close the doors for her, to save her getting out again, but the housekeeper hadn't appeared before Trina had left, so she did it herself, shivering in the icy wind. Then she ducked back into the car and turned it cautiously to go down the long drive to the road.

Enough cars had passed to have created long, almost bare patches in the road, and Trina proceeded with more assurance. It wasn't so bad after all, though heaven knew what it would be like coming home that evening if the clouds let fall the burden they were still so obviously carrying. Still, she'd worry about that when the time came. The important thing now was to get there.

Keeping her speed down and negotiating bends very carefully, Trina found herself making better time than she had dared to hope. There wasn't much else on the roads and she was spared most of the fear of wondering just what an approaching car might be going to do. She felt triumphant enough as she passed the turning that led to Griff's cottage to take her eyes from the road ahead and glance quickly aside, as if mentally thumbing her nose and saying 'so there'.

But her momentary triumph was short-lived. For as she looked, she saw Griff's car approaching from the cottage. It was quite unmistakable—a dark green Volvo, almost filling the narrow lane between the hedges, coming straight at her, large and threatening.

Trina was past almost as soon as she had registered the sight. But not before she had also registered the sight of its occupants—*two* people, she thought dazedly. Griff, big and dark, in the driver's seat. And his passenger—muffled in fur, flame-red hair like an aureole round her face, and sitting closer to Griff than might necessarily have been expected.

Julia Meredith, without a doubt. And it took all Trina's skill in driving to prevent her car going straight into a skid at the revelation. There was only one reason why Julia Meredith could be coming away from Griff's cottage at this hour of the morning. And you would have to be pretty naïve not to realise all the implications in that.

Griff must have gone back to her from Compson House last night. Back to her arms, from Trina's. No wonder he hadn't wanted to complete what he'd started with Trina—he must have wanted to save his energies! And no wonder he hadn't wanted to collect Trina that morning—or to let her go to work alone, risking just such a confrontation as they had almost had.

Sick at heart, Trina drove on to the glassworks almost mechanically. So it had been all a farce; all a dream on her part and a cruel hoax on Griff's. Just what his motive had been, she didn't know. To get her co-operation in the factory, presumably. Perhaps he'd intended to follow up with one of his revolutionary ideas for the future of the firm, confident now of her approval.

Well, it was just as well she'd discovered the truth before committing herself, one way or the other. Her face burned as she remembered the way she had behaved in his arms last night, the way she had almost begged him to complete his lovemaking and take everything she had to offer. He hadn't, and now she was deeply thankful. At least she still had a few shreds of self-respect left.

Not that they'd keep her very warm through the chilly days that lay ahead, she thought as at last she came within sight of the glassworks and sighed with relief that she had arrived safely. And chilly they were certainly going to be. Thermal underwear could keep your body warm, but it wouldn't do a thing for your heart. And the ice had already penetrated there. It would take a very fierce fire to thaw that out again.

CHAPTER SEVEN

GRIFF arrived at the glassworks at two o'clock, and Trina saw at once that he was in a towering rage. She was in her design office when he found her and she looked up and met his eyes coolly, though inside she was shaking.

'And just what are you doing here?' he demanded almost before he was through the door. 'I told you to wait until I fetched you at twelve!'

'You've still quite a lot to learn about me, haven't you, Griff?' Trina laid her pen on the desk so that he wouldn't see her hand was shaking. 'Like *nobody* tells me what to do. Not even you.'

'It was for your own good——' he began, and Trina cut in angrily.

'My own good? Griff, you're not my nanny! *I* can decide whether or not I'm capable of driving my car. And I damned well will! Not that it was entirely the weather that made you want to keep me off the roads,' she added, keeping her eyes on his face. 'There was rather more to it than that, wasn't there?'

The office seemed very quiet suddenly. Griff was perfectly still as his eyes sharpened to gimlets; then he said in a dangerously quiet voice: 'Just what do you mean by that, Trina? Would you care to explain?'

Actually, Trina would have preferred not to; she was already regretting having said so much. But she'd gone too far now to draw back, so she plunged on recklessly. 'You know full well what I mean! If you'd called for me this morning you'd have had to bring Julia Meredith too, wouldn't you? And you knew that if I drove myself I'd risk seeing you with her. And there was only one conclusion to be drawn from that!'

'And that is?'

Trina flushed painfully. That was something she

119

wasn't prepared to go into. 'You know very well what it is,' she muttered.

'I see. You wouldn't require any explanation, then? You wouldn't believe me if I told you that Julia was returning from London yesterday; that she was booked in at the Swan but came out to see me yesterday evening—uninvited and unexpected, I may say—and when she tried to leave her car wouldn't start? You wouldn't believe that it was too late to call out a garage mechanic or that, rather than drive her to Bridgnorth and then come back in that foul weather, I gave her my bed and spent the night on the sofa downstairs? Or that I drove her into Bridgnorth first thing and that my call to you was occasioned by genuine concern for you, and nothing else?'

'Oh, I'd believe one thing in all that, certainly,' Trina retorted, all her bitter jealousy of the older woman flooding up as she spoke. 'That she spent the night in your bed! But nothing else, I'm afraid.'

The silence then was long and tense, heavy with menace. For a full minute they stared at each other and Trina shrank back in her seat, convinced that Griff was about to strike her. Perhaps she shouldn't have said that—perhaps she really had gone too far. But why? she thought rebelliously. What else could he expect? All the evidence was against him, and his only explanations were too feeble and predictable to carry any weight at all.

'I see,' Griff said at last, and his voice was flat and toneless. 'Then we both know where we are, don't we, Trina? I see no useful object in continuing this conversation, do you? Perhaps you'd like to bring me up to date on what's happening this morning?'

Trina heaved a tiny sigh of relief. So it was all going to be forgotten—swept under the carpet. They were going to keep their relationship now on a strictly business footing. Well, that suited her just fine. It was a pity they hadn't done so right from the start.

So why this cold emptiness inside her? Why this aching, as if somewhere inside she was crying bitterly and hopelessly for something of ineffable value, lost and broken beyond repair?

With the help of Robert Nicklin and the Works Manager, John Batten, the new order was organised and set under way. The men took to it with interest, concentrating on the new shapes and designs until they were able to produce them as quickly as the standard lines. The work involved was considerable, particularly in the engraving and cutting rooms, where the machines had to be set up for the patterns to be marked on the glass before cutting. But in a shorter time than Trina would have thought possible the factory was in full production and work went ahead smoothly. There seemed to be no reason why the order shouldn't be met with time to spare.

One of the men most affected by the new order was Trevor, who made the larger pieces. Trina went along on several occasions to watch him at work, knowing that he appreciated her interest, and they would chat as he waited for the gatherer to bring him a fresh 'gob' of metal on the long iron.

'How are the wedding arrangements going?' she asked one morning. 'It won't be long now, will it?'

'A few more weeks—you'd think it was plenty of time, but there seems to be more and more to arrange all the time,' he grumbled. 'Cakes and receptions and bells and choirs and God knows what. Making a proper meal of it, they are! I'll be glad when it's all over. Still, at least they've got somewhere to live. Found a place out Hagley way. Little terráced house, it is—not bad at all. Buying it on a mortgage, of course.'

'Well, that's good news, Trevor,' Trina said warmly, and he nodded.

'It is that. Means they won't be wanting to stay on with us. I'll be able to have the Bride to myself for the first time in twenty-four years!'

Trina smiled. He really was an old softie under that growling exterior! 'You'll be having your silver wedding next year, then,' she remarked. 'We'll have to celebrate that, Trevor.'

The gatherer brought him the iron and he turned away, moving out into the centre of the space around the chair to swing the heavy metal until it was of exactly the right length. It was a process that had never ceased to fascinate Trina as she watched him begin to blow shape into the red-hot glass. It must be almost a sixth sense that told him just when to stop, measuring with huge calipers to see that it was exactly the right size, reheating in the glory-hole, swinging, marvering and blowing again. Each completed jug, bowl or vase was exactly the same as its fellows, yet each one was hand-made, and it was only the skill Trevor had developed over years of practice that made it possible.

Trina returned to the office. She and Griff were working together with a cold, efficient politeness these days, and although it wasn't pleasant it was certainly effective. They spoke to each other only when necessary and each was scrupulously correct in dealing with the other. Trina wasn't at all sure how long she would be able to keep it up, but she was determined to see this order through before she allowed her emotions to take charge again.

The weather continued to be bad, with snowfalls, thaws and then freezing which made deathtraps of the roads. Driving in to work and home again became a nightmare, and although Griff once again offered to pick her up in the mornings and drive her back at night, she refused with a politeness that was as icy as the weather. He tightened his lips with anger, but didn't press the matter, and he didn't offer again. If he had, Trina would probably have accepted, but, much as she disliked the journey, she wasn't going to ask him.

Nothing more was seen or heard of Julia Meredith. Trina still had no idea who she was, in relation to Griff, but felt certain she must be his mistress. Just the kind of woman he'd like, she thought, visualising the elegant redhead in her mink jacket. Not that Trina herself would ever wear a mink—she was definitely anti-fur, though she would accept sheepskin since sheep were also bred for food. But breeding or killing animals for ornamentation was definitely out, and she didn't envy Julia Meredith her mink in the least!

It was about the only thing she didn't envy, though, she had to acknowledge. Somehow the older woman seemed to have everything. Poise, beauty—and Griff. And when she thought that, Trina knew that try as she might, she still hadn't got him out of her system. Maybe never would. Much as he had hurt her, his thin, arrogant face still haunted her dreams and she still woke believing herself in his arms, with all their quarrels forgotten and the future sparkling before them.

It was a shock, then, when Julia Meredith came into the office one day and confronted her.

Griff was somewhere in the factory and Trina was alone in the office when she arrived. She had been sketching out some new ideas for her Seasons range—she had got as far as Autumn now—and she glanced up idly as the door opened, expecting to see Jean with some late post or, perhaps, a tray of tea.

But it wasn't Jean, in her comfortable sweater and skirt, her face placid and smiling and pleasantly familiar. It was Julia, tall, slender and exotically out of place in this mundane environment. Julia, her voluptuous curves revealingly encased in a dress of emerald jersey that made her spun-glass hair look brighter than ever, a titian-cloud about her head. Julia, her china-blue eyes hard in her porcelain features, her beauty marred by the discontent of her pouting lips.

'Where's Griff?' she demanded without preamble. 'I had an arrangement to meet him this morning and he didn't show up. Is he here?'

'Not in the office, no.' Trina was too startled to do any more than make a direct reply. 'I think he's in the factory somewhere.' During the past few weeks she and Griff had, without really discussing it, evolved a certain routine and a tacit agreement as to which decisions should be made by whom. Griff was probably in the glasshouse, but he could equally well have been in the process-shop or over in the customer departments.

'Have him called for me,' Julia ordered.

Trina blinked. 'I'm sorry, that's not really possible. We don't have any paging system—we've never thought it worth installing.'

'You mean you don't have a tannoy, even? You just have to go searching when you want somebody?' Julia's tone was incredulous. 'My God, I knew this place was pretty antiquated, but——' She left the sentence unfinished, and Trina felt her temper begin to rise.

'I could send someone to find him for you,' she offered, but Julia shook her head.

'Don't bother—I don't have that much time to waste. And I half expected it anyway. Well——' she shrugged her shoulders, '—he knows what to expect. We've talked it over enough, and if he doesn't see fit to take the chances he's offered, there's always someone else willing.'

Trina's eyes widened. Julia was being surprisingly frank. Or could she mean something else? Feeling her cheeks turn pink, she dropped her eyes to the desk, then glanced up to find Julia watching her narrowly.

'Or was it your doing?' the older woman asked slowly. 'You know, I'm beginning to think there's more to you than that innocent exterior would suggest. *Did* you persuade Griff against the idea? He's told me how you feel about this place. Was it your idea to get him to turn the offer down? Because if it was . . .'

'I don't have the faintest idea what you're talking about,' Trina told her, bewildered. 'What idea? What offer? And how could I possibly persuade Griff against—or in favour of—anything?'

'You tell me!' Julia stared at her with narrowed eyes. 'But if it *was* you, then I'll know just how to deal with Griff! He's not that hard to talk round, if you know the way—it might well be worth trying again. I shouldn't think your powers of persuasion would be very effective in the long term, however interesting Griff might find you as a novelty.'

Trina still didn't understand her, but she could recognise an insult when she heard one, and she was beginning to get really angry. Slowly she rose to her feet, uncomfortably aware that she was several inches smaller than Julia, and her green eyes glowed dangerously as she spoke again.

'Would you please explain what you're talking about? Then I may be able to tell you what I know about it. At present, it's absolutely nothing.'

Julia turned her head slightly and stared sideways at Trina, her expression dubious. Clearly, she didn't for one moment believe that Trina really didn't understand her. Then she leaned forward across the desk and for a moment she reminded Trina irresistibly of a cobra about to strike.

'Do you really mean to tell me,' she enquired silkily, 'that Griff never discussed with you the idea of my putting money into Compson Crystal?'

'*Money?*' Trina gasped. '*You* wanted to put *money* into Compson Crystal? I don't believe it!'

'No?' Julia gave her another measuring glance. 'Griff never discussed it with you? Never even mentioned it?'

'No, he most certainly did not! And if he had——' Trina paused. Just what *would* she have said if Griff had told her such a thing? She didn't like Julia, it was true—but would she have refused her money, for the firm? So long as Julia hadn't held a controlling interest ... Could she have afforded, could anyone afford, to pick and choose who gave financial support?

'No,' she said slowly, thinking out all the implications. 'No, he never even hinted at it. I had no idea who you were. I thought——' She stopped again, colour flooding into her cheeks, and Julia gave her a quick glance and laughed without mirth.

'Oh, well, that's another story,' she remarked lightly. 'But I do find it strange that Griff shouldn't have taken you into his confidence over this financial offer. After all, you *are* joint Managing Director. I would have thought you'd a right to information like that—a right to make the decision. Somewhat high-handed of him, don't you think?'

'Yes, I do,' Trina answered. She sat down again and

Julia sank gracefully into the chair opposite. 'Er—just when did you make the offer, Miss Meredith?'

'Oh, please—Julia.' The other girl gave her a dazzling smile. 'You know, you and I could be friends, Trina—it is Trina, isn't it? Pretty name. And the firm belongs to your family, I believe. Oh, the offer—well, I don't remember the exact date. Quite a little while ago. We've discussed it quite a lot, Griff and I.'

'And he never even gave me a chance to think about it.' Trina frowned at her desk, littered with drawings. She had thought that Griff and she were evolving a workable relationship, distant though it might be. Now it looked as if he had been fooling her, taking the really important decisions behind her back while allowing her to think that she was totally involved. There was that way he'd gone off to London . . . How could she have allowed herself to think she could trust him?

'Do you mind telling me, Miss Meredith—Julia,' she asked, 'how long you've known Griff? And just why you decided to offer to put money into the firm?'

Julia opened her blue eyes wide. 'How long I've known Griff?' she echoed. 'Goodness me, now you're asking! Longer than I care to admit to, I'm afraid. We've been friends for a very long time. Since he first left Compson's and started up his own studio, in fact. Since the first time he needed finance.'

The words took a few moments to sink in. Trina stared at her visitor and assimilated their meaning. The *first* time he'd needed finance? Then . . . 'Are you saying that you've given Griff money before?' she asked slowly. 'That you helped him with his studio in Herefordshire—put money into that?'

'Why, yes,' Julia answered casually. 'Didn't you know?'

Trina sat back in her chair. So *this* was the basis of Griff's relationship with Julia Meredith! Or part of it, anyway! She'd financed his first effort at independence—helped him, in fact, to leave Compson's and strike out on his own. Had she realised then just what she was doing? And Griff—what had made him accept money from this exotic and elegant woman, so clearly living in a different world from the one he'd been used to? How had they met at all—what had made her *offer* such help?

Well, that wasn't too hard to figure out. She might have come round the factory at some time on one of the regular tours held for visitors to see the glassworks in operation. She could have seen Griff, magnificently male as he wielded the long iron as if it were a spear, displaying the aggressive grace of a jungle animal as he fashioned a beautiful glass object from the molten metal that came from the glowing furnace. Trina herself, a regular visitor to the glasshouse, had seen women notice Griff, watching him rather than the work he was doing. It was only too possible that a woman like Julia, confident of her own charms, would find ways of meeting Griff away from the glasshouse, discovering his talent and his aspirations and encouraging him, all for her own purposes.

From there it was only a tiny step to the idea that if it hadn't been for Julia, Griff might never have left the factory—and everything might have turned out differently.

Julia was watching her, eyes narrowed again. It was as if she had been able to follow every step of Trina's thoughts and her face was cautious. She opened her handbag—real crocodile to match her shoes, Trina thought with distaste—and took out a slim gold cigarette case. Trina shook her head as it was held towards her, and Julia lit one of the slim, dark cheroots and blew smoke expertly.

'You seem upset about something,' she remarked. 'What is it, my sweet? Don't you like the idea of big, macho Griff being beholden to a woman?'

The way she said it, Trina didn't like it at all. Logically, she knew that was silly—but the fact remained that this woman had helped Griff to betray her father, the firm and herself, and whether Julia knew it or not, Trina didn't like it. But perhaps she had known it. The knowledge was unlikely to have made any difference. It hadn't to Griff, after all.

'I'm sorry,' she said stiffly. 'You'll probably think it was none of my business—but I happen to think Griff let the firm down by going independent as he did. Most of our apprentices stay loyal to us and spend their lives here.' It was odd, speaking of Griff in that way. All right, he'd started off as an apprentice—but she had to admit there was a difference. Not that she was prepared to admit it to anyone other than herself.

'But Griff's different, isn't he?' Julia said smoothly, reading her thoughts. 'I mean, deliciously husky as most of your workmen are, they don't have that extra— something—that Griff has. And I must say I've never regretted helping him as I did. He's certainly repaid me in full—and with interest.' Her insinuating tone left Trina in no doubt as to the manner of his repayments. 'That's why I was so keen to help with this new venture. And why I just couldn't understand why he didn't take up the offer—or even discuss it with you.'

Trina passed a hand across her eyes. She didn't understand it either, and she was becoming totally confused. She wasn't even sure now about her feelings towards Julia. Was the other woman simply interested in Griff as a glassmaker, seeing him perhaps as a means to increase her own finances? Or was there more to it than that? And the remarks she kept making in that deceptively silky voice—were they as innocent as they sounded? Or were they intended to have the effect they were having—which was to increase Trina's anger towards Griff?

'I think I'd better get someone to find Griff,' she said. 'He can't be far away. Then we can get this straight between us.'

Julia rose from her chair and picked up her fur from the desk where she had draped it. 'No, don't bother,' she said, slipping it round her shoulders. 'As I said, I don't really have the time. And Griff has made his answer plain by simply not keeping our appointment. I doubt if I'll bother him again. Unless he changes his mind, of course.' She smiled charmingly at Trina. 'You may be able to help there,' she suggested. 'That's if *you're* interested, of course ... Well, goodbye, Trina. So nice to have had this little chat. We really should have done it before, don't you think?' And she drifted out, leaving the air faintly tinged with what was obviously a very expensive perfume, while Trina sat at her desk too bemused to answer.

Well, she thought, sweeping her drawings together in a heap, so *that's* what had been going on! It was no use attempting any more work this morning—she just had to get this sorted out in her mind, get her own thoughts straight. She had to know her own mind before she faced Griff again. But before she could even begin, the door burst open once more and he swept in, dynamic as ever, ready, she could see, to start issuing orders, infuriating her even before he'd opened his mouth.

'Don't say it, Griff!' she exclaimed, getting in first. 'Just tell me what's been going on. What you should have told me weeks ago—what we ought to have discussed between us, instead of it being kept a secret from me until it was too late, as it is now!'

Griff stopped dead and stared at her, his eyes blinking as he tried to disentangle her words. Trina was dismally aware that she hadn't expressed herself at all well, but before she could rearrange her thoughts he was speaking.

'Would you mind re-phrasing that?' he asked pleasantly, making her flush with annoyance. 'I'm sure there must be a meaning hidden in there somewhere, but I've never been very good at cryptic clues.'

'You know very well what I mean,' Trina declared furiously. 'Or shall I give you some more clues? Like— offers of financial help? And Julia Meredith?'

Griff's eyes widened and he sat down abruptly in the chair Julia had only just vacated. 'So that's the way the wind blows,' he murmured. 'I had an idea that was her car I saw driving away. Just what has she been saying to you?'

'Nothing that wasn't true, I'm sure,' Trina retorted.

'And nothing that you couldn't have told me yourself.' She stared helplessly at him. 'Griff, why didn't you tell me Julia wanted to put money into Compson Crystal? You kept on about the firm needing money—even about the possibility of bankruptcy. Why didn't you tell me about this? It ought to have been discussed by the board. You'd no right to keep it to yourself.'

'On the contrary,' Griff returned brusquely, 'I had every right. I'm sorry, Trina, I'm not prepared to discuss it any further than that. The offer's closed now, anyway, as I'm sure Julia will have made clear to you.'

'Closed by your not keeping an appointment with her this morning. Griff, she might be willing to reconsider— she was astounded to find that I knew nothing about it. Look, I don't know whether it's a good idea or not— but shouldn't we consider it? Shouldn't the board discuss it? Just what does it involve anyway? You just can't make decisions like this entirely on your own.'

'In general, you're right. But not in this specific instance. I've told you, Trina, the subject's closed. If Julia hadn't come in here this morning you would never have known a thing about it—a fact which I suspect she was well aware of.'

Trina shook her head. 'I just don't understand it, Griff. You say you want the firm to do well, to continue in production, and then you do this! How can I believe or trust you?'

'You'll just have to try.' He swung to his feet and towered over her. 'If you can't, that's just unfortunate. Now look, what I came in to say was——'

'*No!*' Trina leapt to her feet and banged her fist down on the desk so that her lamp rattled and a pencil jumped into the air and fell to the floor. '*No,* Griff! I've told you before, don't patronise me! I *won't* have my head patted and be told to run away and not bother my pretty little head! I want to know just what's been going on between you and Julia—businesswise,' she added hastily as his eyebrows quirked. 'Or—all right—*any* wise. Maybe it's all tied up together. She told me she financed you when you first left Compson's, and she told me you'd repaid her with interest. What kind of interest—do you mind telling me that? It seems to me that might have some bearing on the whole thing!'

In the ensuing silence she could hear quite clearly the chatter of Jean's typewriter in the adjoining office, and voices and laughter from along the corridor. Presumably they could all hear her, too, she thought dully, and didn't even know if she cared. Nothing much seemed to matter any more.

Griff's eyes had narrowed to chips of glinting stone. He took a step towards her and she shrank back in her chair, suddenly afraid. As he loomed over her, he seemed bigger than ever, a great menacing shadow that could easily swamp her, taking her over, blotting out all conscious thought . . . She blinked up at him, eyes as green as the sea, and raised her hands as if to fend him off.

'You needn't worry, Trina,' he told her, his voice as low as a bass key on a piano. 'I'm not going to strike you. Though I'd like to—I'd like to turn you over my knee and give you all the hidings your father ever should have given you and clearly never did. But this isn't the place, is it?—although it's most definitely the time. I shall have to postpone that pleasure until the two coincide. As one day they most assuredly will.' He paused to allow his threat to sink in, then continued mercilessly, 'You've tried your luck many times and in many ways, Trina, but this time you've gone just a little too far. Don't try again. Just forget what you've just said to me, and forget what Julia said, too. I've told you, there is no discussion. None. Have you got that firmly into your——' he paused '—*pretty little head*? Yes? Then perhaps we can return to the business I came in to discuss.'

His voice brooked no further argument, and Trina subsided. She wanted to continue the discussion but knew that if she pushed any more Griff would, whether this were the place or not, carry out his threat of giving her a spanking. And that was a humiliation she just couldn't suffer. Once again, she thought rebelliously, brute strength had won the day. And she railed inside at the arrangement that had made men stronger, physically, than women. It just wasn't fair, and if she'd been there at the beginning things would have been done very differently.

She was thankful to leave the works early that afternoon to drive home. The sky had darkened threateningly and one or two snowflakes touched her face as she went out to her car. Trina groaned inwardly. Was this long, dreary winter ever going to end? A quotation came into her mind ... *'If winter comes, can spring be far behind?'* Yes, it could. It could be a long, long way behind. So far that it was out of sight and might even have got lost altogether.

She thought of Trevor and his family, eagerly planning their spring wedding. To them, it probably all seemed a good deal closer, with so much to arrange— the church to book, invitations to be sent, food to be prepared. Trevor had told her that the whole family was helping, each making something for the reception and stowing it away in deep-freezers. They were having the reception in the canteen and a lot of Trevor's workmates would be there, as well as friends and relations. It must be lovely, she thought as she drove along the darkened roads into the countryside, to belong to a large, close family. It was the atmosphere she loved in the factory, intensified. Something she'd never really known; her mother's early death had robbed her of brothers and sisters, taken the chances of family life away from her.

And if she had had brothers, probably everything would be different now. Her father wouldn't have brought Griff back into her life, there would have been no need. And she wouldn't have had all these worries and responsibilities that weighed so heavily upon her. She could have continued happily with her designing, a member of the board but with no final decisions to make ...

Trina caught herself up sharply. What was she thinking? That she didn't like being Managing

Director? That she couldn't cope with the job? Surely not—it was just that she was tired and dispirited after the events of the day. And it would all have been so much easier if Griff and she had been on better terms; as she'd thought for a while—such a short, short while—that they could be. Easier too, perhaps, if that brief ecstasy had never been; then she would never have known just what she'd lost.

CHAPTER EIGHT

NOTHING more was heard of Julia and Trina assumed that she had returned to London, or wherever her home was. Griff never mentioned her, and on the one or two occasions when Trina tried to bring up the subject she was met with a cold implacability that chilled her heart and left the words dying on her lips. Clearly, there was to be no discussion of the offer of finance, and Trina seethed with resentment at Griff's high-handedness. Whatever his own feelings, the board should have had the opportunity to consider it, and she wasn't at all sure what the shareholders would think either. Griff had stepped out of line, but what could she do about it? He had only to give her one glance of cold steel and she floundered in confusion. She would never be able to present a convincing case against him.

The attitude of the rest of the board strengthened this conviction. Trina was hurt and annoyed by the way they all seemed to turn to Griff, hanging on his every word. Didn't it matter to them that he'd abandoned the firm years ago and only returned now because he'd been offered an important position? So he was a talented glassmaker—did that make him a good Managing Director? Maybe all that force and energy were going to land them all in trouble, she thought miserably. It could sweep them all along a path from which there was no turning back. She was well aware of the fact that Griff had by no means given up his revolutionary plans for new lines, colour and so on. Once this big Arabian order was complete he would return to them, and with some possibility of getting his ideas across after his success with this.

He seemed to be taking over more and more, she thought as she went through the morning's post. Several letters were concerning matters of which she knew nothing—obviously things Griff had dealt with, without reference to her. So what had happened to their original agreement? Discontentedly, she stared at one of the letters. It seemed to require a fairly quick reply, yet she had no idea what it was about, and Griff was nowhere to be seen. It would serve him right if she simply ignored it and left it for him to find when he did deign to show up—but that could result in a loss of business or goodwill, and that was something she wasn't prepared to risk.

Exasperated, she went to search for him—his Volvo was parked outside the offices, so he had to be around somewhere. She went through the cutting-shops, stopping to look at the work and showing her pleasure in the effect of the designs for the Arabian order. Elaborate and ornate, they were certainly most effective, the lights striking brilliant colour from the minutely cut facets. She picked up a glass, so finely cut that it seemed to be surfaced with tiny diamonds. The two lozenges on the sides had been left blank for the falcon and the desert flower that would be added by the intaglio workers, and she went across to look at the completed glasses. The Sheikh should certainly be well pleased with these, she decided, and congratulated the workers who were producing such exquisite work.

'It's a pleasure to do,' one of the men told her. 'Nice to have something different to work on, and when you finish one of these you really feel you've done something.' He lifted the glass itself, examining it with professional eyes. 'Takes some doing, this design, but it's good.'

Trina went on, her heart lifted by this. These people were artists and craftsmen, taking a real pride in the work they did. That was what made a glass factory so different from any other. Everything was handmade, each separate piece relying on the skill of its makers; there was no mass production here, and when the day's work was ended it was with a sense of satisfaction rather than relief that it was over. And many of the employees went on to evening classes to learn yet more about glass, studying medieval design and other subjects simply out of a deep interest in their craft.

Derek was working on a large bowl as Trina passed and he didn't look up as she paused beside him, admiring the great falcon with outspread wings that was taking shape on the heavy glass. Pictures of the Sheikh's palace and gardens lay on his table too, and she knew that he was practising as much as possible on rejected pieces that would later on become 'cullet' and returned to the batch mixture for melting down and using again.

With a jerk of memory, she recalled that she had actually come to look for Griff, and she hurried on through the process-shop, pausing only momentarily to watch the glass emerging slowly from the *lehr* for inspection and finishing before it was cut. Yes, the order was progressing well. But there was no time to linger. Griff had to be found, and she had plenty of her own work to be getting on with too.

She went through to the glasshouse, pushing open the heavy swing doors. No sign of him at this end. Slowly, with a word and a smile for each of the men, she walked past the various chairs, noting automatically what each was doing. Glasses—tumblers—dishes—her mind ticked off each item as she passed. And then she rounded a corner to the casterole chair and stopped dead.

Of Trevor there was no sign at all. But the chair was in full operation. And the man at the centre of it, swinging the iron, blowing, shaping the metal from a heavy, molten lump of red-gold to a graceful, finished shape of clear lead crystal, was Griff.

Trina watched in an astonishment that turned rapidly to anger. What in God's name was *he* doing here? Where was Trevor? And what—just what—did he think he was making?

There was nothing she could do about it. Griff was entirely concerned with the glass he was making, and to approach him while he was engaged upon difficult work would have been foolish and dangerous. She could only stand by, fuming, and take in the scene before her eyes.

At first she thought that he must be making one of the large bowls, and she bit her lip in vexation. That was *Trevor's* province—large pieces were his speciality and it was the height of discourtesy for a Managing Director, however skilled, to elbow his way in and take the man's work from him. She would have something to say about this once Griff had finished, that was for sure! But as she watched the glass take shape a doubt crept into her mind. If Griff was really making a bowl he was making an unexpectedly poor job of it. The object that was emerging on the end of the iron was little more than a shapeless mass, not even rounded, totally unrecognisable. What had happened to Griff's famous talent that he could make such a mess of it? And that was valuable raw material he was mistreating, too. It would be fit only for cullet by the time he'd finished with it.

Trina wanted to stop him, wanted to wrench him away, but she knew she must do no such thing. Until he had finished whatever it was he was trying to do, she was helpless.

Worse still, none of the other men in the chair seemed the least bit concerned. In fact, she realised in amazement, they seemed downright *interested* in what Griff was doing—gathering round to watch as he swung the iron with an expertise that spoke of long practice and plunged it into the glory-hole to reheat the cooling glass and make it malleable again. Their eyes never left the glowing shape as he rolled it again and then stood still, holding the iron vertically so that the amber mass drooped and lengthened like a fiery tongue; judging the exact moment when it would have cooled sufficiently to retain its shape, he sat down quickly in the chair and snatched up a wooden patten to shape the sides, patting and stroking with deft movements to perfect the form he was aiming to achieve.

But what *was* it? And the men—couldn't *they* see that it was an utter disaster? Why on earth didn't one of them *say* something? Griff might be joint M.D., but these men had known him as an apprentice and none of them was the type to mince words. They were craftsmen themselves, it must be hurting them even more than it was hurting Trina to watch the distortion that was taking place.

The glass was now a rigid, glowing flame, heavy-based, its sides wavering to a rounded taper, With the utmost care, Griff laid it on the board and tapped sharply on the iron so that the glass snapped cleanly away, leaving a flat base that would need only minimal smoothing. He stood for a moment regarding it, evidently satisfied. It had taken longer to make than any piece Trina had ever seen and apparently demanded a higher degree of skill and concentration. She stared as it was taken away to the annealing *lehr* for cooling. What on *earth*—and then, with a flash of revelation, she knew.

It was one of Griff's own pieces of glass—the modern 'glass sculpture' with which he had made a name for himself in Herefordshire. The kind of glass Trina had fought against allowing him to make here; the kind of glass that was against all Compson's tradition, ornamental rather than functional, as shapeless as a piece of toffee allowed to run from an upturned saucepan and—in Trina's opinion—no more artistic.

Her fury was running at about the same temperature as the glowing furnace when Griff finally handed the glass over to be taken to the *lehr* and turned towards her. But even then she couldn't speak her mind; the men were clustered round him, laughing and clapping him on the back. They seemed to *approve* of what he'd just done! And a deep disappointment in the men she had thought she knew so well mixed with her anger and inflamed it. Without pausing to consider, unable to hold back her rage a moment longer, she stepped into the circle and faced him.

The men fell back a little, making way for her. They glanced at her blazing green eyes and the laughter died out of their faces. But Trina was past caring what any of them might be thinking. She lifted her face towards Griff and met his dark eyes with a burning green gaze. She had forgotten why she had come looking for him, forgotten everything except what she had just seen. All she could think of was the need to make it clear to Griff exactly what she thought of him.

'What the *hell* do you think you're doing?' she demanded. 'What was that—that *deformity* you've just perpetrated? You don't seriously believe you've made an object of beauty there, do you? It's just about the finest example of wasted time and wasted metal that I've ever seen! Cullet, that's all it's fit for, and when it comes through the *lehr* I shall make it my personal business—and pleasure—to see that that's just what it is!'

'Oh no, you won't,' he retorted, his eyes glimmering. 'It's taken me half the morning to get that glass just right and there's no way you're going to get your hands on it, now or when it's finished——'

'*Finished?*' Trina yelped. 'You mean there's *more* time and skill to be wasted on it? What on earth do you propose to do to it next? And you say it's just right? However can you tell?'

'I'll ignore that piece of sarcasm,' he grated. 'You quite obviously don't know the first thing about glass sculpture——'

'Thank the lord!'

'—but *I do*. I also know there's an increasing market for it——'

'We've been through all this before. We don't need that market.'

'And that's a matter of opinion, only in your case opinion seems to be a synonym for prejudice!' Griff stared at her in disgust. 'My God, what have I done, to be landed with a reactionary little traditionalist who can't see more than an inch in front of her spoilt little face! I tell you, Trina, as I've told you before, our only hope is to branch out. We've got to be ready to try new ideas, and I'm the one who can do that——'

'Mr Modesty himself!' she taunted him. 'However did we manage all those years without you? Be your age, Griff. You've just been playing this morning—that *thing* you've made is nothing more than a frigger, just a variation on the pieces apprentices make for fun. There's no use or sense in it, and if there *is* a market for it, then the people who buy such idiocies must have more money than sense, that's all I can say. But that's not the main thing,' she went on, oblivious now of the ring of flabbergasted faces that surrounded them. 'The main thing is your total lack of responsibility in taking Trevor off his chair to waste time and money in making such rubbish just when we're at our busiest time, just when we ought to be working flat out to get the order done for the delivery date. What's got into you, Griff—have you taken complete leave of your senses? Don't you realise how important this work is—or are you trying deliberately to sabotage it, is that it? What in——'

'Trina, for God's sake stop acting like a fishwife and be quiet,' he broke in roughly. 'You have no idea what you're talking about, but if you'll just stop haranguing me for a minute or two, maybe I can tell you. The piece I've just been making——'

'Oh, don't bother, I don't want to know! I'm not *interested* in your toys, Griff, all right? Just so long as no more time is wasted on them.' She glanced quickly round at the men, flushing as she met their embarrassed eyes. 'And where *is* Trevor, anyway? He ought to be working on this chair. Don't tell me you've taken it upon yourself to move him?'

'No.' Griff's voice was dangerously quiet. 'Not quite. I simply gave him the morning off. He——'

'You *what*?' Trina whirled on him, eyes snapping with renewed fury. 'You gave him the morning off? Why? I thought it was understood that there would be no time off except in emergencies? Just what's going on here, Griff Tyzak? Have you had a shareholders' meeting without my knowledge? Are you sole Managing Director now? Because you're acting like it! Or do I still have some small say in what goes on in *my* factory?'

Griff sighed. 'Don't be childish, Trina,' he ordered sharply. 'And might I point out that this is *not* the place to hold our arguments?' He glanced at his watch and spoke to the men. 'All right, you might as well have your baggins now. We'll carry on afterwards.' He watched as the men disappeared, muttering uncomfortably between themselves as they did so. 'I should imagine that did a great deal for the morale of the works,' he commented ironically. 'Right—now let's get a few things straight——'

'That suits me! Like who's actually in charge here and just what your game is—why did you give Trevor time off, for instance? So that you could have your little play, presumably. Is the—the *toy* for Julia, perhaps? A little present? My,' she jibed, 'you must think I'm nothing but a puppet—but I'm not going to dance to *your* string-pulling, Griff Tyzak! I have as much say in the running of this place as you do, and don't you forget it!'

'I'm not likely to get the chance,' he rasped. 'And now, if you've had your say, maybe you'll allow me to get a word in. First of all, Trevor came to me and asked for the morning off. He might as easily have come to you, except that you weren't available just then and I was. Secondly, if he *had* come to you, you would have done exactly as I did and given him the morning off. Only if you had, time *would* have been wasted, because this chair would have either been idle or having to make ordinary glasses, whereas I've been able to put the time and the men to good use——'

'*Good use?*' Trina squeaked, but she was able to say no more as Griff took one step towards her and, before she knew what was happening, had one arm firmly round her shoulders and a hand clamped tightly over her mouth. Struggling was useless; she put all her fury into her eyes and glowered at him over the restraining fingers.

'To continue,' he went on inexorably. 'As I said, you would have done exactly the same. Trevor needed the time off to go and sort out some difficulties over the house his daughter and her fiancé are buying. The deposit had to be put down at once and they couldn't get it together before next week. Trevor wanted to go to his building society, get the draft and pay it over to the solicitor. I couldn't refuse and neither would you have done. If I had, they would have lost the house.' He removed his hand and Trina rubbed her bruised lips. 'Anything you'd like to say?'

Trina shook her head speechlessly, and he went on, turning slightly away from her to fiddle with an iron that was leaning against the furnace. The glasshouse was empty now, the clatter silenced. Only a forgotten transistor radio played somewhere in a corner.

'Right. Now the piece of glass I was making. It's not just a whim of mine, nor is it a waste of time, manpower or metal. That piece is part of the order. I told you that Mohammed had bought a couple of my pieces already. When he discovered my position here he ordered three more pieces—all of glass sculpture—to be made as a wedding present from himself to his sister. It seemed only commonsense to use the time when Trevor wasn't here to make them, the men in his chair being the most experienced and the most able to help. *Now* do you have anything to say?'

Trina shook her head blindly, her eyes misted with tears of humiliation. Once again, he'd won. And not only that—he'd allowed her to make a complete and utter fool of herself in front of the men. The story of the row would go all round the factory, and she could just imagine what they'd be saying. That she wasn't up to the job ... that Griff Tyzak ought to be sole M.D. .... Oh, God! She covered her burning face with her hands. It was all his fault, she told herself savagely. He ought to have told her about Trevor—about the glass—and he should never, never have let her dig her own grave like that in front of the men!

'Well?' Griff demanded mercilessly. 'Don't you think you owe me an apology, Trina?'

Trina's hands dropped away from her face like stones as she faced him. 'An *apology*?' she gasped. 'An apology? What for? For not being psychic? For not being around when Trevor wanted to ask for time off? For not knowing that your precious Mohammed had given you an extra order? No, Griff, I don't think I owe you any apology at all. In fact, I find your motives highly suspect. Just why didn't you tell me about that extra order? Just why did you go about it in this—this furtive manner? If I hadn't happened to come to look for you this morning I might never have known about that misshapen, misbegotten atrocity that you're pleased to call art! So what's the real purpose behind it? Not just a wedding gift, I'll be bound. No—you want to present me and the board with a *fait accompli*—you want to show us this monstrosity, tell us it was actually ordered and then demand that we make more. Turn the whole factory over to them, perhaps. Oh yes, it's easy to see your reasoning,' she continued bitterly while Griff stood watching her, his face dark with anger. 'There'd be nothing we could say, would there? We'd have to give in. Or maybe I'm wrong,' she added, as a new thought struck her. 'Maybe it isn't that at all.'

'Oh?' Griff enquired sarcastically. 'And what other horrific motive are you ascribing to me? I'm all agog to hear.'

'You've still got your studio in Herefordshire,' Trina said slowly. 'Maybe you're simply drumming up business for that? And when you've used Compson Crystal to bring you more customers, maybe you'll desert us once again and take them all to Tyzak's. Yes, that makes sense. Either way, you're the winner, aren't you? Or so you think.'

'It certainly looks like it,' he agreed with a sneer. 'And once you start looking for treasonable offences there's no end to what you can dig up, is there? Fortunately, everyone is not so suspicious as you are, dear Trina. You saw the way the men were co-operating with me this morning. I can command co-operation of that sort throughout the factory, and I intend to. *They* understand what I'm trying to do. They also understand the difference between ability and nepotism!'

The crack of Trina's open hand across his cheek was like a gunshot in the quiet glasshouse. Horrified, she stepped back, staring at her scorched palm in disbelief. It had been a purely involuntary reaction, arising out of sheer fury—but if she'd given it long and careful thought, she knew she would have done just the same.

'That was unforgivable!' she panted, retreating from the blaze of anger that irradiated his lean face. 'Don't touch me, Griff—you deserved it, and I'll do it again if you come near me!'

'Chance would be a fine thing,' he gritted as he grasped both her wrists in steel-hard fingers, holding her far enough away to prevent her kicking his shins. 'I wouldn't struggle if I were you—you'll only get hurt. Now, let's try to get a little sense into you. At least I know the way to tame that temper of yours—don't I? . . .' And before she could protest, he jerked her hard against him, bent his head and laid his lips upon hers in the hardest, most demanding kiss she had yet experienced, his teeth bruising her soft mouth as arms of iron crushed her against his hard body and the breath was forced from her lungs. She struggled, but her struggles were feeble and ineffective; and they faltered and died as the old power surged through her body, the power that Griff had always had to turn her will to water, and she felt her blood begin to heat in her veins and her heart to swell and tighten as her breasts were swelling against him, and her legs to lose their strength so that she was forced to cling to him with both hands.

All her memories came rushing back; Griff's passion and his tenderness as they lay before the fire on the night he had brought her champagne and told her about the order; his gentleness when she had confessed that she loved him, his refusal to take advantage of her desire, telling her he wanted an old-fashioned romance. . . . Bitterness swamped her heart at the thought. There had been no romance, old-fashioned or otherwise; nothing but unhappiness and hatred and a continual battle against his attraction.

And now there was no sign of that tenderness in his touch. His lips burned her skin and she could taste blood from the cruelty of his teeth on her mouth. His hands were hard and ruthless on her body and she knew that there would be bruises to show for the encounter by the time she undressed that night. Yet in spite of this she could sense a deep hunger in him, a hunger that surely matched her own, and she knew that although his kisses were occasioned by anger there was still something less harsh buried in his heart; deeply buried, she thought with despair, too deeply ever to come to the surface again ... even if she wanted it to.

It seemed an eternity before Griff released her, so suddenly that she staggered, and gave her a thrust that sent her out of his reach. Tremulously she glanced up at him, and caught an expression of such intense disgust that she recoiled. So once again her instincts had played her false! There was no desire for her, no gentleness, in Griff Tyzak. She had been deluding herself, and maybe it was just as well that she realised it. For there was no room for tenderness in the relationship between them. The things he had said to her could never be forgiven—neither could his brutal way of ending any argument. Nor the way he had behaved over the factory. No—any feelings she might still have for him, in spite of all that had happened, must be buried as deeply in her as his feelings were buried in him. They must never be allowed to come to the surface. Not if she were to survive.

She backed away, keeping her green eyes fixed on his, hoping that he could see the loathing on her face, and said in a trembling voice: 'Don't you ever dare to do that again, Griff Tyzak! I don't want you to touch me again, ever. I wish I needn't see you—but since I have to, let's keep our meetings as brief as possible, shall we? Until they don't have to happen any more.'

Before Griff could ask what she meant, she had turned and run through the glasshouse, feet avoiding steam-hoses and broken glass as nimbly as a mountain goat avoiding rocks and crevasses on the path of a glacier. She reached the door and flung it open just before the men returned from their short break, thrusting her way through them, hardly noticing their astonished and concerned glances. Then, blessedly, she was in the open air and away from them all.

If only she *could* be, she thought, shuddering in the biting air and stepping carefully on the icy path. If only she could get right away, away from the worries and cares—and away, especially, from Griff Tyzak. But that was impossible, as long as she stayed here at Compson Crystal. And she wondered briefly whether she could face a lifetime here, fighting this incessant tug-of-war with the arrogant man whose presence had been imposed upon her so unexpectedly. It was survival of the fittest—and she wasn't at all sure, just now, that she had the stamina or the strength to stand out against him. So far, she hadn't been very successful; he had won just about every round of the battle between them. How was she going to cope if it went on like that, as surely it would?

Every fibre of her being revolted against the idea of leaving Compson Crystal, abandoning her inheritance and letting Griff Tyzak take complete control. It could surely never have been her father's intention that such a thing should happen. But just what *had* his intention been? She had still never really understood why he'd wanted Griff to have so much power in the factory. If only he'd told her, explained—but he hadn't had the chance. He must have meant to talk it over with her, give her his reasons—but there had been no intimation that he would die suddenly, relatively young. He must have been waiting for what he considered the right moment before he told her.

And that moment had never come. Perhaps the right moment never did—you had to just go ahead to do what you felt was right, before it was too late. However unpleasant or embarrassing it might be.

Trina sighed and went back into her office. Jean had been in while she was gone and left a pile of neatly-typed letters on the desk among the post Trina had left scattered when she went to look for Griff. She bit her lip as she stared at the mess, remembering the letter she had thought sufficiently urgent to cause her to search for him. She hadn't even mentioned it, and she found it now, crumpled and grubby, crammed into her pocket. So she'd have to find him this afternoon and give it to him then. Just when she would have been glad *not* to have to seek him out again, too.

The door opened and she glanced up to see Derek coming in, carrying something large and bulky. Her heart lifted. Perhaps Derek's undemanding presence was what she needed, perhaps he could comfort her battered pride. He hadn't been able to before, a small voice remarked in her head, but she quickly closed her mind to doubts. Derek was kind and he was fond of her, and what more could she need?

'Hullo, Trina,' he said, settling his parcel down on he desk. 'Sorry I couldn't speak to you this morning. I thought you might like to see the reason.' He pulled off the paper like someone unveiling a plaque, and Trina gasped with delight.

'Derek, it's beautiful! It must be one of the best things you've ever done.' She let her hands touch the huge bowl, her fingers moving reverently over the great falcon engraved on its side, every feather of its outstretched wings delicately outlined, its legs shaggy and its beak and talons razor-keen. 'It's absolutely perfect, Derek,' she told him sincerely.

'I'm pretty pleased with it,' Derek admitted. 'I'll tell you something, Trina, this big order's brought new life to the works. Not just because it means work—but it's so good to be doing something different, trying new designs, new shapes even. I'm not saying we'd got into a rut lately, but we haven't done anything really new for a while, have we?'

Trina stared at him. *Derek*, wanting to try new things? But of course he just meant new patterns, new styles, didn't he? He wasn't talking about radical change.

'I've been working on a new range,' she told him. 'Based on the seasons. We'll start thinking about it once this order's out of the way. . . . But you're not feeling stale, are you, Derek? You do freehand work—surely you don't get bored with that?'

He lifted his shoulders. 'Well, one eighteenth birthday goblet's much like another,' he said with a grin. 'You can get tired of engraving Christian names, too. . . . I've really enjoyed doing this bowl, Trina. I'm looking forward to the rest of the order, too—the one with the palace on the side, and those pieces of Griff's.'

Trina's head came up sharply. 'Pieces of Griff's? What pieces are those?' As if she didn't know, she thought angrily, and Derek looked at her in surprise.

'Why, you know, those sculptures he's making. I believe he was going to do the first this morning— didn't you see it? I'm hoping to make a start on it soon. Now that will be something new—I haven't engraved anything like that before. And it's not just the engraving, you know—half the effect is brought about by actually chipping tiny pieces of glass off the back of the piece to make faceted reflections. The Swedes do it marvellously, of course. But there's no reason why we shouldn't corner a bit of the market, is there? Griff's done so already——'

Trina broke in, unable to bear this eulogy any longer. 'Derek, are you serious? Do you honestly mean to say that you *approve* of this—this so-called sculpture? You *want* to work on it?'

'Yes, why not?' Derek nodded, blithely unaware of Trina's mounting indignation. 'As I said, it'll be something new. And the engraver works in much closer co-operation with the maker. I mean, he's the one who's visualised the complete piece. He'll need to do any work on the shape itself, and the engraver puts the picture on either the front or the back of the piece, according to the effect that's wanted.'

'You—you seem to know all about it,' Trina said faintly.

'Yes. Griff and I have gone into it quite deeply.' Derek seemed to notice her expression for the first time. 'I say, what's the matter, Trina? You're looking quite washed out. Not feeling off colour, are you?'

'No, I'm quite all right,' she managed through stiff lips. 'Derek——'

'Are you sure?' he persisted. 'I mean, there's a lot of 'flu about—and I wouldn't mind betting you've had no lunch. You don't look after yourself, Trina. Let me call Jean—or would you like the nurse to have a look at you?'

'I told you, Derek,' Trina said through gritted teeth, 'I'm quite all right. I just wish——' But what she wished Derek never learned; for at that moment the telephone rang, making them both jump.

Exasperated, Trina snatched it up and answered it curtly. Then her expression changed; her face whitened so that her eyes looked like brilliant green jewels and even though she was sitting down she swayed, gripping at her desk for support. She seemed to be listening for a long, long time, and when at last she spoke it was merely to say 'Thank you' in a voice that was no more than a thread of sound, before she replaced the receiver carefully in its cradle.

'What is it?' Derek exclaimed in alarm. 'Trina, for heaven's sake, what is it?'

The flames had died out of Trina's eyes, leaving them dull and heavy as she stared back at him. But she didn't answer—she couldn't tell him what she had just learned. There was only one man she could tell, and he wasn't here.

'Find Griff Tyzak for me,' she muttered through dry lips. 'Get him here at once—*please*, Derek!'

Derek hesitated for one second, then took another quick look at her face and left the office at a run. Trina sat at her desk, staring unseeingly at the bowl which had only a few moments before given her such delight. Slowly, she reached out her fingers and traced its shape, the shape she had designed, the shape she had watched form from a lump of molten glass under Trevor's expert touch only a few days ago.

Where the hell had Griff got to? And why hadn't Derek found him? She got to her feet and paced the office, covering her face now and then as a sob shook her slim body, letting the hot tears fall unheeded to the carpet. Oh God, what a thing to happen—what a cruel, callous joke! Who was it who arranged these things? Why did they have to happen?

The office was no longer large enough to hold her grief and her anger. Crashing the door open, she stormed out into the passage and through the door which led to the yard. If Griff had been in the factory, he'd come this way ... She stared across, aware of the snow that was falling once more and cursing it with all her heart. The factory spilled yellow light from its windows and she could hear the noise of the glasshouse, the clatter of irons, and the whine of the cutting wheels. Where was Derek? And where—*where*—was Griff?

And then she saw him. His huge figure, outlined in a doorway as Derek pointed across the yard. The turn of his head as he put some question, the shrug of Derek's shoulders as he confessed himself unable to answer it. And then she could wait no longer; she began to run across the yard, straight for Griff, straight for that big body which had given her such comfort and such torment.

There was no comfort there for her now. She stopped a yard short of him, panting from her run, her breasts outlined by the thin sweater she wore under her thick knitted jacket, and her green eyes flamed at him with a passion greater than she had ever known before.

'All right, Trina,' Griff said mildly. 'What's the problem? Surely it's nothing that can't be solved. Calm down and tell Uncle Griff all about it.'

At any other time his words would have inflamed Trina's anger even more, but now she hardly noticed them. Her eyes glistened as she stared at him, fighting for breath, and he moved a step closer, his expression changing to one of concern. But as he reached out a hand to support her, she jerked herself away as if his touch might be contaminated.

'Just keep your hands off me, Griff Tyzak!' she blazed at him. 'I told you never to touch me again, remember? And listen to me—I've just had a phone call. From the hospital in Hagley. Trevor's been involved in an accident. Some fool skidded on the ice and went straight into him. Both cars are a write-off and Trevor's badly hurt. Do you hear that, Griff Tyzak? Our best worker—and my friend—lying badly hurt in hospital, and *it's all your fault!*'

'All *my* fault?' Griff echoed. 'How do you make that out, Trina?'

'Of course it's your fault,' she railed at him, her tears breaking through in full force now. 'You gave him the morning off, didn't you?—not because he needed it, but just so that you could use his chair to make your precious piece of sculpture! If you hadn't, he'd be here now, working, happy, making plans—instead of lying in a hospital bed, badly injured and perhaps never able to work again. Of *course* it's your fault—but you won't see that, will you? Nothing you do is ever wrong— nothing!' She turned away, choking, unable to speak another word, and offered no resistance when she felt a pair of arms take her gently by the shoulders and lead her back to her office. Derek, she thought gratefully, accepting their support. She ought to have known she could rely on him. Especially in a crisis like this.

'Have your cry out,' a voice said softly in her ear. 'Let it all out—that's right—you'll feel better for it. I'll get Jean to bring some tea and then I'll get on to the hospital again and find out just how bad things are. Here—have a hanky.'

Trina accepted the hanky and soaked up the tears. It was large and comforting. But it wasn't Derek's—and neither were the voice, nor the arms that had supported her across the yard.

Griff Tyzak, she thought hopelessly as the tears flowed, and she didn't know whether they were for Trevor or for herself. Griff Tyzak, who somehow *always* managed to be in the right.

CHAPTER NINE

THE tea Jean brought helped Trina, and she dried her
eyes to find Griff on the phone, saying little, his face
serious. When he replaced it at last she watched him
with wide, questioning eyes, and he shrugged slightly.

'They can't really tell for sure yet,' he said, 'but he
seems to have multiple injuries and a lot of cuts. Hadn't
fastened his seat-belt, apparently, and went through the
windscreen. They'll be able to tell us more later—he's
gone down for X-ray now.' He reached for his tea and
swallowed it in one gulp. 'God, what a thing to
happen!'

'What about his family?' Trina asked dully. 'His wife
and daughter? And he's got two sons too—one's at
university, Aston, and the other one's still at school.
Trevor was hoping to sign him up here as an apprentice
in the summer.'

'His wife knows and she's on her way there.' Griff
hesitated, his eyes on Trina's tear-stained face. 'I was
wondering if you—but not if you don't feel up to it, of
course——'

'If I what?' She caught his meaning and jumped up.
'Of course I'll go—so long as I'm not butting in. She
may have someone with her, they're a big family—but
I'd like to be there. Just——' her voice wobbled, '—just
in case——'

'I'll drive you there now.' Griff was cool and
competent, taking charge without fuss. 'Put your coat
on, Trina, and finish that tea while I tell Jean. And then
I'll come straight back—there's a lot to think about.'
He touched her shoulder gently as he passed. 'Heart up,
Trina. It may not be so bad as it seems.'

And it might be worse, she thought dully as she did
as he'd told her and pulled her duffle coat round her.
Even if Trevor pulled through, he was going to have to

spend a long time—maybe months—in hospital. And what then? Glassblowing was heavy, strenuous work. Would he be able to return to it? Or would he have to spend his days doing light work, checking for faults in shape and pattern, watching other men do the work he had been so skilled in, his pride shattered along with his body?

She hardly spoke as Griff drove her to the hospital. Snow was falling thickly now and the traffic was moving only slowly, held up frequently by cars which had become stuck, unable to negotiate slopes or sliding terrifyingly across the road, their sideways slewing motion as unpredictable as the scuttering of crabs. Trina sat with her hands clenched into fists on her knees, silently cursing every other driver on the road and wondering why she had never felt pleased and excited to see snow falling. It was beautiful but cruel, and she would never be able to see it again without remembering this terrible day.

They reached the hospital at last and Griff came in with her. It seemed to take an eternity to find out where Trevor was; the girls on the reception desk were clearly harassed and overworked, and one of them told Trina that they had been admitting the victims of road accidents all day. 'It's been a nightmare,' she said. 'Trevor Hodgetts, did you say? Yes, he's in Ward Twelve. Follow the green line.'

'I'd better not come with you,' said Griff as Trina turned to go. 'The car's on a yellow line. Ring me and let me know what's happening, won't you? I'll come back later.'

Trina nodded, her nerves too taut to allow her to speak. Stomach churning, she set off through the long, bleak corridors, following the green line painted with the other coloured stripes on the floor. They seemed to go on for ever; how did anyone ever find their way around this mausoleum? The smell of hospitals, a mixture of disinfectant, boiled fish and other, less identifiable odours, assailed her as she went, and every now and then a hurrying nurse passed her; once she had to stand aside as a bed trundled by, pushed by a young man in a white coat. She seemed to have walked miles before she finally arrived at Ward Twelve.

'Yes, Mr Hodgetts is in this ward,' the young nurse told her, consulting a list. 'But he's not having visitors at present. His wife's in the waiting-room, if you'd like to join her.'

Trina went along the corridor to the waiting-room and found Trevor Hodgetts' wife sitting alone in a small armchair. She looked up quickly as Trina entered, her face a mixture of hope and fear; but when she recognised Trina, the hope died away, leaving only the fear.

'Mrs Hodgetts, I'm so sorry.' Trina crouched in front of the dumpy little figure of Trevor's 'Bride' and took her hands. 'I had to come. Do you mind?'

The grey head shook and the misted brown eyes wavered as the older woman clutched Trina's hands as if they were a lifeline. 'No, of course I don't mind, Miss Trina. It's good of you to bother.' The voice trembled as she added: 'Our Marjorie was coming, but her youngest was sent home from school and she couldn't . . . It's nice to have someone here.'

Trina took the seat next to her and they sat in silence. There was nothing one could say, she thought miserably, wishing she knew how to comfort the bewildered woman next to her. But anything she said would be false.

'Has there been any more news?' she asked after a while, and Mrs Hodgetts shook her head.

'No—they've been X-raying him. Said they'd let me know as soon as they could.' Footsteps sounded in the corridor, quick and light, and they both looked at the door. But the steps went on by without pausing. 'It all takes such a time. And all because someone skidded. He was killed, you know, the other man. They said my Trevor was lucky to get out alive.' Her voice broke and she buried her face in her hands.

Trina sat helpless, her arm around the woman's shoulders. God, what a mess! And the other man—

whoever he was—did his wife know yet? Were his family already shattered and mourning, their lives changed for ever by one false move behind the wheel?

'It was good of you to come,' Mrs Hodgetts said, pulling herself together. 'I'm sorry about this—I just don't seem able to help——' Her voice broke again. 'Trevor always thought the world of you and your dad,' she said.

'We've always thought a lot of him too,' Trina said soberly. 'He's one of our best men, you know.'

'And Mr Tyzak, too. He's a good man, Trevor says. Mr Compson did right to bring him in.'

An odd little pain lodged itself in Trina's heart. Was this really what Trevor thought? Would it still have been his opinion if he could have seen what Griff had done that morning? And a dart of anger struck her. She was still convinced that the blame for Trevor's accident could be laid fairly and squarely at Griff's door.

This time, the footsteps stopped outside the waiting-room. Trina and Mrs Hodgetts were half on their feet before the nurse had the door open, eyes wide with anxiety; they watched her as she stood there, willing her to give them good news.

'Mrs Hodgetts?' The nurse gave her a professional smile. 'We've finished the X-rays. Your husband has a few broken bones, I'm afraid—three ribs, and a fracture of his right leg. And his face is rather badly cut, but that will all heal. You can come along and sit by his bed, if you like.'

'Is—is he conscious?' Mrs Hodgetts asked in a whisper, and the nurse shook her head.

'I'm afraid not, and we won't really know everything until he does regain consciousness. There's no fracture of the skull, but there is concussion, and we won't know how serious the effects of that are until he wakes. It would be nice for him to find you there then.'

'Yes—I'll come.' She turned uncertainly to Trina, who said quickly: 'I'll wait here, Mrs Hodgetts. Mr Tyzak said he'd come back for me later—I'll stay until then, at least.' She wouldn't be wanted in the ward, she knew, but at least Trevor's wife would know that there was someone familiar in this great building. At least she would be within call.

The dumpy, grey-haired little woman went out with the nurse, leaving Trina alone with her thoughts. And there were enough of them to last her for a long time—certainly until Griff came back a couple of hours later, to find that Trevor had still not regained consciousness. By then his daughter Carol and her aunt Marjorie had arrived; and Trina, suddenly exhausted, left them still waiting.

She made no objection when Griff rang the next morning to tell her that he would collect her for work within half an hour. She had little heart for objecting, even if she'd wanted to. Trevor's accident seemed to have changed everything, though she wasn't sure yet just what the changes were. She only knew that petty squabbling had to be shelved while he lay so ill.

Petty squabbling? Was that really all that her constant differences with Griff had been? They had seemed so important, so vital—were they really nothing more than petty squabbles?

'Have you rung the hospital?' she asked before Griff rang off, but he said no, they had told him to ring at nine.

'We'll do it as soon as we get to the factory,' he said, and Trina wondered if Mrs Hodgetts had spent the night at her husband's bedside. Had he recovered consciousness? And if so, what had his waking revealed? Was the concussion serious, would he be damaged in some way, or would he simply have a bad headache? If only she could *know*! And as she thought that, Trina had a flash of sympathy for the woman whose anxiety must be so much greater.

Griff said very little as he drove to the factory and Trina sat gazing out at the whitened scenery. Rather to her surprise, she found that she could still appreciate the beauty of the snow, even while she recognised its perils. The fields were blanketed as if wearing duvets, and she remembered being told as a child that snow was good for the crops, keeping them insulated from frost. Last night's fall still lay like a mantle on the hedges, and the trees were outlined in fleecy white. The clouds had cleared away, leaving the sky a tender blue, and a pale winter sun sparkled on the white landscape, sending a million tiny rainbows flashing across the shining smoothness. In one sloping field a small crowd of children were already out with toboggans, their anoraks and woolly hats bright spots of colour, red, blue and yellow, looking like the tiny figures on a Christmas cake.

'What are we going to do?' she asked suddenly. 'The factory—the order—Trevor will never be well in time to complete it. Those big pieces, the bowls and vases. . . .'

'Is Trevor the only workman capable of making them?'

'No—but he's certainly the best. And if we put someone else on his chair—Mike Barrett, for instance, or Steve—it means their teams will be held up. Well, there's no help for it—they'll just have to make glasses, we'll all have to do the best we can, I suppose. If only time weren't so short!' She stopped as Griff slowed down to negotiate a slippery stretch. 'Let's hope nobody else has an accident,' she added fervently.

Griff lifted the phone as soon as they were in the office and dialled the hospital. He was put through to the ward at once and Trina watched his face anxiously, conscious of Jean standing beside her but unable to do more than give her a quick glance of greeting.

'I see,' Griff said expressionlessly. 'Yes, I'll see to that. Yes. Thank you. This afternoon?' He rang off and looked at them.

'What did they say?' Trina demanded urgently. 'For God's sake, Griff, don't just stand there! Tell us—how is he?'

And then, just as she was beginning to fear the worst—that Trevor hadn't come round, even that he might have died—Griff's expression relaxed. He had been anxious too, she realised belatedly, and unable to

respond immediately to the news he'd been given. Now
a dazed grin appeared on his face and he said in a
husky voice: 'It's all right, Trina. Trevor came round
soon after midnight. He's got the mother and father of
all hangovers, but there's nothing worse than that. No
brain damage—just a few broken bones. He's going to
be all right!'

'Thank God,' Trina whispered, and collapsed into
her chair.

Half an hour later, warmed by a mug of coffee and
feeling better than she had for twenty-four hours, she
looked up at Griff and repeated the message he had
given her—a message from Trevor himself. 'He wants
me to go in and see him? Really? What about his wife?
And the rest of his family?'

'Mrs Hodgetts will be in bed, getting some rest, if she
has any sense,' Griff told her. 'And young Carol, too,
probably. They were at that hospital until the small
hours. And they'll be going in to see him again in the
evening. No, it's you he wants to see, Trina. Or at
least——' he hesitated, '—it's actually both of us. But
you'll have to go alone this time. I'll drop in later.'

'Why? What will you be doing?' Trina felt a small
flare of hurt and indignation. What was so important
that Griff couldn't leave it to go and see Trevor?

'Apparently one of the things that's bothering Trevor
is the fact that work on the order is being held up,'
Griff told her quietly, and she felt ashamed. 'I want you
to reassure him. Tell him it's going ahead just as
planned; tell him it isn't being held up at all.'

'You mean we're going to put Mike or Steve on it?
That won't satisfy Trevor for long—he knows it means
other production will be slowed down——'

'No, I don't mean that.' Griff stood up and held her
eyes with his own. 'I mean I shall be taking over
Trevor's chair, Trina. From now on, I'll be the gaffer
on those big pieces. Hospital visiting will have to be
done out of working hours. And I think Trevor will
appreciate that.'

'*You?*' Trina whispered, and the room swayed around

her. 'You're going to do *Trevor*'s work? But——' Her
words faltered into silence and Griff smiled rather
grimly.

'I *am* a trained glassblower, Trina,' he reminded her.
'I actually worked on the casterole chair before I left,
and I've done quite a bit of the same kind of work in
my own studio. I think I can probably cope.'

'Yes—yes, of course, I didn't mean——' She didn't
really know what she had meant. A confusion of
thoughts whirled in her brain. Would Griff really be
able to cope? And what about the work here—the work
they were supposed to share? Panic welled up in her and
she raised frightened green eyes to his. He was still
watching her, and his eyes still had that sardonic,
cynical coldness that chilled her blood. It was as if he
could read her thoughts—as if he was waiting for her to
say that she couldn't cope without him. Well, that was
something she couldn't admit! Gathering her tattered
dignity around her, she said coolly: 'That sounds an
ideal solution—for a stopgap, anyway. You won't
attempt anything you're not sure of, will you? And yes,
I'll go and see Trevor this afternoon.' Her voice
wavered as she added simply: 'I'm glad he's going to be
all right.'

Griff nodded curtly. Her barb about not attempting
anything he wasn't sure of, coupled with a reference to
a 'stopgap' had not escaped him, but he said nothing as
he set down his own coffee-mug and picked up his
jacket.

'I'll start right away,' he said flatly, and Trina
nodded. She was bleakly aware that their recent truce,
caused by Trevor's accident, had been only temporary.
Oh, it would probably last as long as necessary—until
the present emergency was over—but underneath it all
there was still the same undercurrent of hostility; still
the same, endless battle between them.

Trina spent the rest of the morning working in the
office. She went through the mail, including that which
hadn't been dealt with yesterday; dealt as best she could

with the ones that were obviously meant for Griff, dictated replies to Jean and made phone calls. By lunchtime she was exhausted, but she refused to have more than a mug of soup and a sandwich at her desk, and worked doggedly on.

'I've got to go to the hospital soon,' she told Jean when the secretary remonstrated. 'If I leave this now it'll be all the worse tomorrow. Griff isn't going to have time to cope . . .' She wondered just what Griff was doing in the glasshouse. Making the bowls that Trevor would have been employed on, or using the time to produce another of his sculptures? She sighed. They were, as he had pointed out, part of the order, so she would have to accept his making them. So long as they were the only ones. . . .

Just before three a taxi arrived to take her to Hagley. Griff had forbidden her to drive herself, and indeed she couldn't have done so since her own car was still at home. 'I'll go straight home after I've seen Trevor,' she told Jean as she picked up her bag and coat. 'See you in the morning.' She went out to the taxi, wishing that she'd had time to go across to the glasshouse. It would have been nice to have been able to tell Trevor exactly what was happening.

Once again she followed the green line to Ward Twelve; once again she spoke to the young nurse on duty in the tiny office by the door. But this time she was allowed in. And the first person she saw was Trevor, half sitting up in bed, bandaged and white, but looking better than she had dared to hope.

'Trevor!' Relief put a scolding tone in her voice. 'Well, you are a fine one, aren't you? Scaring us all like that. . . . How are you feeling?'

'Not too bad,' he admitted. 'Bit weak. And it hurts to laugh, with these ribs. But I wanted to see you—to tell you I was sorry.'

'Sorry? What for?'

'Well, for taking the morning off. Oh, Griff said I could go—I didn't just skive—but I feel I've let you down, landing up here with things as they are.' His face was strained as he looked at her. 'What about that big order, Miss Trina? Is it going to be messed up because of me?'

Trina looked at him. His face was swathed in bandages, he was clearly uncomfortable with his ribs strapped up, and one leg encased in plaster. He must be in pain, yet he was worrying about his work and about the factory. She felt a rush of warm affection for him and all the other men like him. And she was more determined than ever not to let Griff, probably at this very moment making some more of his strange pieces of glass, jeopardise their future.

'No, nothing's going to be messed up, Trevor,' she assured him, making up her mind to visit the glasshouse first thing in the morning to make quite sure that Griff was doing what he should be doing. 'Everything's going on just as it should be. We miss you, of course, but we'll manage.'

'Who's on my chair, then?' The worry was still there in his eyes. 'Michael's not bad, but you have to watch him a bit. Or Steve, now, he's a good lad ...'

He was beginning to move restlessly, giving grunts of pain, and Trina laid her hand on his arm. 'Don't get agitated, Trevor,' she said softly. 'I told you, everything's all right.' Or had better be, she thought grimly. 'Griff's taken over your chair—he's going to stay on it as long as necessary. Nobody's been moved, so production hasn't been upset at all. You've nothing to worry about, nothing at all.'

'Griff?' Trevor stared at her. 'Griff's taken over? Well, why didn't you say so?' The tension drained out of him as if a plug had been removed, and he sagged with relief. 'Phew! That's a worry off my mind, I can tell you! Griff doing my job!' He shook his head and to Trina's astonishment began to laugh, stopping abruptly as his ribs pained him. 'That's a turn-up for the book, that is! Griff Tyzak, on my chair!'

'I'm glad you're pleased,' said Trina, just a shade stiffly. What was so funny about it, she had no idea. 'Do you think it'll be all right? He can do the work?'

Trevor stopped wheezing and looked at her in surprise. 'Well, of course he can! No question of that. Don't you realise, if he hadn't left he'd have been on that chair now? That was his pitch, and I'd never have got further than making wine-glasses.'

'Oh, that's nonsense!' Trina exlaimed. 'You're an artist, Trevor, you'd never have been kept making glasses. Dad wouldn't have allowed it.'

'He might not have had that much choice.' Trevor leaned back against his pillows. 'There's only room for so much talent in a works like Compson's, and if there's more than you can handle the men either stay back or leave. Griff left—if he hadn't, I'd have stayed back on the wine-chair. I'd have had to, see? I wouldn't have left Compson's.'

'No, I don't believe you would. You've got real loyalty.' Trina spoke softly, but Trevor gave her a sharp glance and snorted.

'Loyalty's nothing to do with it. I'm just not the type to start up on my own. Couldn't cope with it all, could I—all the business of finding a studio and worrying about rent and money for materials and all that. No, that's not for me—I'm no businessman. I'm just a glassmaker, and that's enough for me. There's designing, too—thinking up new ideas for shapes and patterns. I couldn't do all that.'

He paused for breath, and a nurse came round with a trolley and offered him a cup of tea. Trina sat watching him, shaken by his words. He was right, of course—you had to be more than an artist to make a success of independence. That still didn't put Griff in the right.

'No, Griff was right to move on,' Trevor continued, setting his cup on the locker. 'And your dad saw that, too. Give him his due, your dad was never one to hold anyone back. Anyone with any ability got all the chances he needed, and if he didn't choose to take them—well, that was his affair. But Griff took 'em. And your dad was right behind him, all the way.'

'How—how do you know all this?' Trina asked.

'Used to talk to me a lot, Griff. Well, we did a lot of

our training together. He was younger 'n me, but he learned fast—soon caught up. In his bones, see? Well, he come to me one day and asked what he ought to do. Knew he wanted to do more than he could at Compson's, see, but he didn't feel right about just up and leaving. He had these ideas about loyalty, like you said just now. I told him what I thought.'

'And that was?'

'Why, to go to your dad and tell him how he felt. Oh, I know that most apprentices, most workmen too, wouldn't have thought of doing that—but your dad had always taken a special interest in Griff—dunno why. Saw the talent in him, I suppose. He didn't come from round here, you know, Griff. Came from down in Wales somewhere, though you wouldn't think so from the way he talks. Told me once his father was crippled and he had to do the best he could for him and his mum. I guess that's why he wanted to branch out, see if he could make a bit more for them.'

Trina felt cold. Could all this be true? There was surely no reason why Trevor should be making it up. She opened her mouth to speak, but Trevor was saying something else, his voice weaker now, and she bent her head to listen.

'I reckon your dad could see farther through a brick wall than most of us. He knew that if Griff went away he could develop himself more—and then, when he came back, he'd be more use to Compson Crystal. And that's how it's worked out, see? He knows all the business side of it, he's a better glassmaker than anyone in the works, and he's not afraid to try something new. Yes, it was a good day for Compson's when Griff Tyzak came back.'

He leaned back, breathing painfully, and Trina noticed with alarm that his pallor had deepened. As he closed his eyes she got up and looked around, a little desperately, for a nurse. Luckily, there was one nearby, chatting to another of the patients, and she came over at once.

'It's all right, he's just tired,' she said quietly, her

competent hands making Trevor more comfortable. 'He shouldn't have talked so much, only he seemed so anxious to see you. I hope everything's all right? It was his work he was worrying about.'

'Yes, it's all right. I don't think he'll worry any more.' Trina took a final look at Trevor. It hurt her to see his strong frame helpless and bandaged in the hospital bed, but at least it seemed clear that he would be able to return to work once his fractured bones were healed. She thanked the nurse and turned to leave the ward.

Trevor had given her quite a lot to think about, she reflected soberly as she went out to the taxi. It seemed a pity that she hadn't known these things before. And she wondered just what else there was for her to know.

But there was really no time for thinking during the next few days. The work in the office seemed to pile up around her ears, despite Jean's help, and there was never a moment to go into the factory. Trina sat toiling away at her desk, day after day, growing increasingly frustrated. She saw little of Griff, who came in only after the men had gone home, and did some work then. But after the first week he announced that they would have to do overtime, and then Trina saw nothing of him at all.

'I really must get down to the glasshouse tomorrow,' she told Jean, pushing her fingers through her hair as they dealt with yet another pile of correspondence. 'But there's that meeting with the wholesalers tomorrow morning, and I suppose they'll expect lunch, and then in the afternoon Mr Bratten's coming—I can't see when I'll have a moment. I never dreamed there was so much to do in this job! Dad never seemed to be in the rush I'm in.'

'He'd been doing it for years,' Jean reminded her. 'But I shouldn't worry about the glasshouse, Trina. Everything's going smoothly there, by all accounts. Mr Tyzak stepping in like that made all the difference.'

And that was something she might almost rather not have known, Trina thought, savagely attacking another letter. Not that she actually wanted things to go wrong—far from it—but why did it have to be *Griff* who was the hero of the hour? There'd be no holding him at all when all this was over, she thought ruefully. Having proved himself and won the respect of the men, he would be less than willing to take second—or even equal—place with her.

And why should he, after all? For little though she might like the fact, he *had* proved himself, hadn't he? If the men respected him, he had earned that respect. Rather more than she had with her tempers and her shouting matches with him, both here and in the glasshouse.

Hot colour swarmed into her cheeks as she remembered that last encounter with Griff, when she had found him making his glass sculpture. She'd screamed at him then like the fishwife he'd called her, oblivious of the men who stood around, shocked and embarrassed. What kind of impression could she have given them of herself? Hardly a good one. No wonder they were all glad Griff was in a position of authority— they would hardly have had confidence in her after that little exhibition.

And it hadn't been much better here, in the office. Again, she'd lost her temper and hadn't cared who heard her. Every suggestion Griff had put forward she had treated, not only with scorn, but with suspicion, as if really believing that he was out to sabotage the firm.

Well, she had actually thought that at one time. But she'd been wrong about other things, hadn't she? Julia Meredith, for instance. She'd suspected all kinds of things where Julia was concerned, yet nothing had been seen or heard of the elegant redhead since she'd left the office—oh, when was it? Weeks ago? Years ago? Somehow, time seemed to have taken on a different measure just lately.

Sighing, Trina pushed all the letters together in a heap. If she were to pay a visit to the glasshouse—and she must, if only to satisfy her own curiosity—it would have to be today. The post would have to wait. Jean had plenty to be getting on with—and maybe half an hour out of the office would do her good.

As always, the factory was alive with noise—the scream of the cutting wheels vying with the clatter of the glasshouse as Trina opened the door between the two. She had walked fairly quickly through the departments, giving only a quick nod as various people glanced up at her. For the first time, she felt truly uncomfortable in the factory. Just what were they all thinking? she wondered as she walked by, barely pausing to examine the new pieces as they stood waiting to be packed. That Griff should be allowed full rein? That she should resign her position and return to the design office? That idea was almost attractive; Trina had been missing her design work and would have liked nothing better than to slough off the worries of responsibility and have nothing more to think of than how best to represent Summer in glass . . . But that was impossible. She was a Compson, and there was no question of abdicating her responsibilities, was there?

As she approached the casterole chair, her steps slowed. She didn't want Griff to think she was spying on him, but she wasn't at all sure that she wanted him to see her. She stopped in the corner and stood quietly watching.

Griff had evidently been working hard all morning. He was stripped to the waist and his rippling muscles glistened in the fiery heat. He was working with the other members of his chair in the smooth rhythm of men who know exactly what to expect of each other, taking the long iron, swinging it effortlessly around, shaping and blowing, knocking the finished article cleanly from the end, when the taker-in carried it carefully to the *lehr* for annealing. There was barely a pause then before Griff, wiping his gleaming brow and flicking back that dark hair, took the next iron from the gatherer and began the process all over again.

Trina watched as he made a large bowl, shaping it perfectly just as she had envisaged it in her design. It gave her an odd feeling to see him making something that she herself had designed. Something that had first taken shape in her mind, been translated to a drawing, considered carefully for its weight and measurements, and finally brought to reality here, under Griff's sensitive hands. Hands that had been just as sensitive when they had stroked her body, slipping an old tracksuit back from her shoulders, cupping her breasts, bringing a singing joy to flesh that had never really understood what love was before. . . .

The flush on her cheeks had nothing to do with the furnace as she shook herself angrily. What on earth was she thinking of? Nothing, on earth, a tiny voice said in her brain—it was heaven she was thinking of. Oh, this was too much! Was she going to remain a victim of this man's power all her life? Was she always to be prey to sensual thoughts and feelings, just because she saw him stripped to the waist in the glasshouse? And why drag love into it?

Because love's what it's all about, the little voice told her. You told Griff once that you loved him. And nothing's really changed, has it?

Dispirited and shaken, Trina turned away. She had found out what she'd come to find out. Griff was, indeed, making the large pieces that Trevor would have made. Wasn't that enough? Did she have to suffer this revelation too?

But if it hadn't come then, it would have at some other time. Truth will out, she thought as she made her way back across the yard to her office. You couldn't go on deceiving yourself for ever. And she might as well face up to the fact that she did, in spite of everything, still love Griff Tyzak.

So what was she going to do about it? From Griff's behaviour, if he ever had loved her she had killed it. And he had never actually said he did, had he? Even that night when he had brought the champagne and they had lain together in front of the fire, he had never actually used the word love.

Trina went into her office and closed the door. The time had come to think very seriously. For the good of the factory—and for her own peace of mind. Because as things were now, it had to be one or the other. And Trina knew that they were both essential.

She was still at her desk when Griff came in, much later, after the factory had finally closed down for the night. He came in frowning, as if wondering who had stayed in the office so late, and his frown deepened when he saw her. Trina looked up and met his eyes without flinching. This time, she'd determined, there would be no shouting, no arguing. Indeed, there was nothing to argue about. Any resistance Griff offered would surely be no more than token. He wouldn't really want her to change her mind.

'Trina?' he said. 'What are you doing here at this hour?'

Trina looked at him. His face was almost haggard in the harsh light and she remembered that he had been working overtime now for a week or more, making heavy glass vases and bowls. He had also been coming into this office each evening to keep up with what she had been doing, and had taken the trouble to leave her notes telling her she had done well, or giving advice on more difficult problems. And after that, she had heard from Mrs Hodgetts when they had met at the hospital one afternoon, he had been dropping in to see Trevor on his way back to the cottage—where, presumably, he had to cook his own evening meal.

'What are you doing?' he repeated, his voice rough with fatigue.

'The same as you, I imagine,' she replied equably. 'Working. And I wanted to see you, Griff.'

'Oh, what about?' He dropped into a chair and reached for a pile of papers. He really did look exhausted, but then so probably did every other man in the factory. Glassmaking and decorating was hard work for all concerned. 'Couldn't it wait?' he added. 'I haven't really got the energy for any more dramatics.'

Trina flushed, but she knew the jibe was deserved. 'I'm not going to cause a scene, Griff,' she said quietly.

'I just wanted to tell you—I'm resigning. I've realised you'd do a better job for the factory on your own. Dad was right to bring you back. But I don't think he ever meant it to be like this. He must have known I'd be better at design than management. So that's what I'm going to do—go back to design.'

Griff's head came up, his weary eyes as dull as pebbles as he stared at her. 'You're joking,' he said flatly, but Trina shook her head.

'It's no joke, Griff. But quite a few things have happened lately to make me think. And I'm sure I'm right. You'll run Compson's better alone than with me holding you back. You'll be able to try out all your new ideas. It's not really my scene. I'd be happier, as I said before.'

'It'll never work. You won't be able to keep out, once you've been in. You'll be constantly objecting to changes. You'll cause more trouble out in the factory than you do here.' Griff shook his head. 'It's not on, Trina.'

'It'll have to be on. Oh, I'll stay until things are back to normal—until Trevor's back and you can take over properly. But after that—you're on your own, Griff. Don't pretend you won't prefer it.'

'I've told you,' he began, beginning to sound angry now, 'you'll never be able to sit in that design office and mind your own business. You'll be in here creating a fuss half a dozen times a week. Look, Trina, you may not like the idea of management, but you made it clear enough in the first place that you intended to be in there with both feet, making the decisions and carrying the can. You can't opt out just because we've hit a rough patch. What about all that talk of loyalty? *You* have loyalties, too—loyalty to the firm, loyalty to the men. Don't you think it's a bit cowardly to duck out just because you don't like the temperature of the water?'

'But I'm not!' Why could he never, never see her point of view? 'Griff, it's *because* of my loyalty to the firm, *and* to the men, that I want to do this. We're tearing it apart between us, and it can't go on. *One* of us has got to go—and the past few days seem to have proved pretty conclusively that it's got to be me. All right, I'll accept that. Because I *love* Compson's—not because I'm chickening out. Can't you understand that?'

Griff stared at her for a long time. Then he said quietly: 'And will you be able to do that, Trina? Will you really be able to sit in that design office and accept my rulings? Even when you don't agree with them?'

Trina took a deep breath. 'It won't come to that, Griff,' she said, getting up and slipping her arms into her duffle coat. 'It won't happen that way. Because I won't be *in* the design office. I told you I was resigning. I meant I'd be leaving altogether. I'm going to do as you did, Griff—branch out on my own. There must be scope for a freelance designer. Maybe it'll be the beginning of a whole new career.'

She was past him and out into the corridor before he could move. As she hurried across the yard she thought she heard the scrape of his chair as he thrust it back. And it was definitely his voice that she heard calling her name as she scrambled into the car and slammed the door.

But she didn't look back as she drove out of the yard. She'd promised herself and Griff that there would be no scene. And that was one promise that she wasn't going back on.

CHAPTER TEN

TRINA drove home in a welter of confused emotion. There was relief in having made a decision at last; relief that, once the present crisis was over, she would be able to turn her back on the bewildering see-saw of her relationship with Griff; relief that she would no longer have to fight him for what she believed to be right, no longer have to see him each day, watching his thin, haunted face and his sensitive hands, loving him and knowing that her love could never again be expressed, that she had killed any chance of his returning it.

And mixed with her relief was a sharp pain which was also to do with never seeing Griff again. What would it be like to live her life without him? Could she really go through her days knowing that she wasn't going to see him, talk to him? It was like facing a journey across an empty, arid desert, with no guarantee of ever reaching an oasis. It seemed that whatever she did must result in pain—it was just a matter of choosing the most bearable.

There was Compson Crystal, too. Never in her blackest nightmares could she have envisaged leaving Compson Crystal. It had been her life, it contained the history of her family. How could she cut ties that were so strong—what would it do to her?

Trina remembered what Griff had said—that she owed her loyalty to the firm and the men. He had implied that her decision had been made through cowardice. But that wasn't true—she'd taken a long, hard look at herself and at him and she'd seen that to carry on as they were was to set a course for disaster. It was Griff who was keeping the firm going, with his dynamic energy, his ability to lead the men, and his undoubted skill, amounting almost to genius, for working glass. It was Griff whom the factory could least afford to lose. If Compson Crystal was to be run by only one of them, that one must be Griff.

And he'd certainly been right in saying that Trina would find it impossible to work in the design office with him in charge. Her nature just wouldn't allow her to accept his changes without argument, and the situation would rapidly become impossible again. No, she had to leave—get right away—cut all connection.

The idea hurt unbearably. But if she had any loyalty towards the firm at all, she had to put up with the pain. And, unconsciously, she lifted her chin and stared grimly ahead through the windscreen. People have survived worse, she told herself without conviction. Though just at that moment she couldn't really recall any actual examples.

Overlying all these emotions, she was conscious of an intense weariness. The strain since her father had died had been considerable and she wanted nothing more than to rest her head and sleep, knowing that nothing more would be required of her. The first thing she would do once all this was over, she promised herself, would be to have a holiday. Somewhere far away from the Midlands of England—far away from England itself. Somewhere warm and exotic, where nobody had ever heard of glassmaking, where she could lie all day on silver sands, swim in a turquoise sea and think of nothing, nothing at all. . . .

She stumbled twice on the way from the garage to the house, not really sure whether it was tiredness or ice that caused her to slip. Not really caring. Only let her get these next few weeks over, and she could start looking forward again. She would have to; it would be too painful to look back. . . .

'You're looking worn out, Miss Trina,' Mrs Aston said as Trina came through the front door and sank down on to a chair, resting her head against its back before she began to take off her boots. 'It's too much for a girl like you, that job. And Mr Tyzak not being able to take it off your shoulders, too, working the way he is. . . . It's a crying shame, that's what it is!'

'Can't be helped, Mrs Aston,' Trina told her. 'We're working to a deadline. It's Trevor's accident that's really made things difficult. That couldn't have come at a worse time.'

'How is he?' Mrs Aston took Trina's duffle coat and hung it up. 'Coming along nicely, I heard at W.I.'

'Yes, he is, thank goodness. Should be out in plenty of time for the wedding. In fact, I don't think he'll be in hospital much longer—they've done more or less all they can and he's just got to rest now until the bones heal.' Trina shivered. 'He was lucky really. When you think what could have happened—what happened to the other man . . .'

They were both silent for a few minutes, thinking of the man who had been killed, leaving two small children for his wife to bring up. It hadn't really been anyone's fault; just a patch of treacherous ice and the bad luck of being in the way. Life could be turned upside down in a moment, Trina thought, and not often for the better.

'I'll have my supper in the library, if there's a fire,' she said. 'Not too much, Mrs Aston. I'm not really very hungry.'

'You've no appetite at all these days,' the housekeeper remarked disapprovingly. 'That's no way to keep up your strength, picking at your food.'

She went off to the kitchen and Trina crawled upstairs. A hot bath would be nice, and then supper in her fluffy dressing-gown in front of the library fire. Maybe then she'd be relaxed enough to sleep properly. That was another thing she hadn't been doing much lately. . . .

Trina did feel marginally better when she came downstairs after her bath. She couldn't really understand why she felt so exhausted all at once. Perhaps it was because she had begun at last to shed her load, had relaxed the taut nerves that had been all that kept her going during these past weeks. But the hot bath in scented water helped, and she had washed her hair too and blow-dried it into a soft cloud of silver around her

head. Then she had wrapped herself in a long silk
nightie that was all frills and flounces in a pale
aquamarine, covering it with a fluffy dressing-gown in a
deeper shade of the same colour.

That felt better. It made a change from trousers and
sweaters and she enjoyed the sensation of silk against
her skin. She felt feminine again—a feeling she hadn't
had much lately. Perhaps the world wasn't so bad a
place after all.

Quietly, she slipped downstairs to the library. Mrs
Aston would probably have left her supper there on the
small hot-tray she often used, and then gone out for her
evening with her sister, as she regularly did. Trina had
the house to herself. Giving a small sigh of relief, she
opened the library door. . . .

The library was lit by one small lamp on a table, and
the leaping flames of the log fire. The hot-tray was
there, with several covered dishes on it. But what drew
Trina's eyes was the table itself. The lamp cast a small
pool of light over its polished surface. And in that light
glowed two objects; both glass; both finely decorated.
But apart from that they were generations apart.

One was the Compson Chalice, its dark blue and
white glimmering in the soft light. The other was a tall
chunk of clear crystal, shaped like a flame on its heavy
base. A piece of glass that had taken skill, concentration
and sheer artistic flair to fashion it from its molten state
to this bizarre shape that looked almost as if it were
molten still, about to flow like viscous treacle, malleable
and tractable yet temporarily frozen in this beautiful
form. . . .

Trina only half registered the word she had used
when a movement caught her eye, and she jerked
around to find Griff lying back in one of the deep
armchairs. He was watching her, his expression
enigmatic in the flickering light, the planes of his face in
the half-shadow gaunt and hollowed. He looked totally
at ease, yet alert and watchful; like a jungle cat, relaxed
but ready to spring at a second's notice.

'What—what are you doing here?' Trina asked, her

mouth dry. 'And why have you taken the Chalice from its case?' Indignation came to her rescue, lending strength to her voice. 'Come to that, *how* did you take it out? That case is kept locked.'

'Then you must have forgotten to lock it for once. Burglary isn't one of my accomplishments.' He was still watching her, and Trina felt all her relaxed nerves begin to tighten up again. She passed a hand over her face. Wasn't he *ever* going to leave her alone?

'But why?' she repeated in a whisper. 'Why have you come—and why did you take out the Chalice?'

Griff came to his feet in the single lithe movement of a tiger. He moved over to the table and she noticed mechanically that he must have been back to the cottage before coming here; he was freshly-shaved, smelling of some tangy lotion, and he had changed into a pair of black slacks and a polo-necked sweater. Standing there in the firelight, tall and slender-hipped, with the sweater tight across his broad shoulders, he looked almost devilish, and Trina took an instinctive step back.

Griff laughed harshly. 'Don't worry, little girl. I'm not a big bad wolf, come to eat you up. . . . No, I just decided that the time had come for a showdown. I was hoping it could be left until a better time—but you've pushed me into it, I'm afraid, and as they say, there's no time like the present.'

'I don't know what you mean,' Trina said faintly. 'I told you, I'll be leaving as soon as Trevor's back at work. You won't have to worry about me any more. I'll be out of your way—you can run things just as you like, and nobody will stop you.'

'My God, Trina!' he expostulated, so suddenly that she jumped. 'Is that really what you think I want? To have Compson Crystal all to myself? Haven't you seen *anything* through those pretty green eyes in these past weeks? Has it all gone over that wilful little head of yours?'

'Well, what *do* you want, then?' Trina cried, stung. 'That's all that's got through to me, I can tell you!' She remembered her vow not to cause any more scenes, and sobered down. 'Anyway, that's not why I made my decision,' she went on more quietly. 'I believe it will be best for the firm if I go. Compson's don't really need me to carry on—they *do* need *you*. It's as simple as that.'

Griff stared at her, then ran long fingers through his thick black hair. 'And what about me, Trina?' he asked softly. 'Don't my needs count for anything?'

Trina stared at him, but before she could open her mouth he had turned abruptly away, gesturing towards the table. 'Look at those two pieces of glass,' he said harshly. 'Tell me what they mean to you—if anything? Just tell me, Trina.'

With an uncertain glance at him, Trina moved towards the table. She hadn't the faintest idea what he was getting at, but it seemed sensible to go along with him; he was in a strange mood tonight and there was a suppressed violence about him that scared her. Standing at the little table, she lifted the Chalice and gazed at it, as she had gazed at it so many times before.

'Well?' Griff asked again. 'What is it telling you, Trina? Just what *is* that piece of glass to you?'

Trina gave him a quick glance. Was he mocking her? But his face was grave, his eyes narrowed chips of glittering agate. She bit her lip, not wanting to express her feeling to that piercing gaze, but she knew that until she did he would show her no mercy.

'It—it's the Compson Chalice,' she began hesitantly, still not quite sure what he wanted to hear. 'It was made in the early days of Compson Crystal and it's been handed down through the family ever since. It—it represents all that Compson Crystal is—beauty, craftsmanship, skill in design and execution.' Gaining confidence now, she went on a little more firmly. 'To me, it's a symbol of everything I've always believed Compson's stands for—unity in the firm and the production of things that are useful as well as beautiful. It's a kind of talisman; so long as we've got the Chalice nothing much can go wrong.'

She finished on a note of uncertainty again; uncertainty, not of what she had been saying but of how Griff would take it, whether he would even understand. She put the Chalice back on the table and gave him a tentative glance, but his expression hadn't changed.

'And now the other piece, Trina,' he said quietly.

Trina bit her lip. Why was he *doing* this—couldn't he see he was torturing her? She turned reluctantly back to the table and reached out to touch the second piece of glass. It felt smooth under her touch, its shape like flowing water, rounded yet with curious little bumps and undulations that made her fingers want to explore further. . . . Half-consciously, she let them move over its surface, exploring its shape, cupping her palms around its curved sides, feeling the slight roughness of the engraving on its back. Slowly, aware of its weight, she lifted it and let her eyes travel over it as her fingers had done.

It was the piece she had watched Griff making in the glasshouse on the day Trevor had had his accident. It was tall and smooth, with a heavy base, and the glow of the fire gave it the same tawny colour that it had had before it cooled. It had been engraved on the back, so that the design showed through the glass like a picture seen under rippling waves. Trina turned it this way and that, catching the fireglow on it; not striking with brilliant colour as a sharply-cut piece would have done, but returning the light softly and tenderly, its hues muted.

The engraving was of a horse. It was a wild horse, for there was no suggestion of placid domesticity about this rampant creature, rearing on haunches that seemed to quiver with power, muscles rippling with sinuous strength through its slender body to give force and vigour to the hooves that beat the air above its head. Every hair of the flowing mane and tail was outlined with strokes that looked almost impossibly delicate, and the shape of the glass seemed to contain the horse like its own miniature world. If it were once to escape from its crystal cage, there was no knowing what would happen, Trina thought, fascinated.

'Tell me about it,' said Griff, and, although his voice was quiet and soft as brown velvet, Trina started and almost dropped the glass. She had been so absorbed that she had momentarily forgotten his presence. But although he brought her back to the present, he did not break her mood, and this time she found it easier to answer him.

'It's beautiful,' she said in a soft voice. 'I never realised. . . . I could look at it for ever. And touch it— it's beautiful to touch, too. It makes me feel— comforted. Yet *he's* not comfortable—the horse. He's wild and free and unpredictable. Untameable, I'd say— yet if you did manage to tame him, what wonderful times you would have. . . .'

'Yes,' said Griff, and Trina gave him a quick look. Was he thinking that those words could apply to a man as well as a horse? Quickly she went on.

'It's a lovely thing, Griff. I was wrong to call it the names I did. It seems to stand for its own principles. Freedom, untrammelled, exuberant. . . .' She stopped again, embarrassed. 'I—I can't think of any more to say.'

'You've said all that you need.' Griff reached out and took the glass from her and she saw how carefully he handled it. 'Freedom . . . yes, it does represent freedom. But it's a freedom that's encased in crystal, Trina. The little horse can never escape from it. He lives in glass— just as you and I do. We can't break free, either.'

Startled, Trina met his eyes and saw that they were brilliant with the need to make himself understood. She drew back a little and said breathlessly: 'But I'm not breaking free, Griff. I'm not giving up glass. I told you, I'll still go on designing.'

'I'm not talking about that only,' he said. 'You're trying to break free of me, Trina, and you can't.'

She caught her breath. This was going too far . . . he had her trapped, here in her own home. . . . Desperately she glanced at the door, but he shook his head.

'Oh, no,' he said, 'there's no escape there. Trina, I didn't come here this evening to make small talk. I came to get this situation cleared up once and for all. I had hoped it could wait—at least until we'd got this Arabian order out of the way. But I can't take the risk of your disappearing from under my nose.' He moved closer. 'Don't you realise, Trina, there's far too much between us for you to do that? We'd both be lost for the rest of our lives. Don't you know that?' He took her gently by the shoulders and kept his eyes fixed firmly on hers.

Trina felt like a rabbit with a stoat. She could no more have moved, or even taken her eyes from his, than she could have flown. Yes, she wanted to say, I know all that, but it only applies to *me*. Not to you. . . . You don't care?

Or could she be wrong about that?

Her heart kicked painfully as he drew her closer and she felt his breath on her face. Then he drew her closer and she closed her eyes, but he didn't kiss her; and, not knowing whether to be relieved or disappointed, she opened them again.

'It's time you knew the truth, Trina,' he said. 'Oh, it's nothing disreputable, don't look so worried! But you mustn't make any decision before you know—about me and about the Chalice.'

'The *Chalice*? But what can that have to do with us—with *you*?'

'Just about everything,' he said, and drew her down into the armchair with him; and, still half dazed, she allowed him to hold her. It seemed right, suddenly, right and natural, and she knew she could resist no longer. 'If it were not for that Chalice,' he went on, 'I doubt if I would be here.'

Trina stared at him. 'What do you mean? That you only came here tonight because of the Chalice? I don't understand——'

'No, I don't mean that.' He raised a hand to stroke back a wisp of pale hair. 'I mean I doubt if I would ever have come to Compson Crystal—or stayed here.

Because that Chalice is a part of *my* history, too.' He looked down at her. 'You don't really know very much about it, do you, Trina? You know that it was one of the first pieces made by Compson's and you know that there are no other pieces by the same maker in existence. But that's all you know, isn't it?'

'Yes, it is. What more is there to know?'

'What more, indeed!' He gave a short laugh. 'Only the name of the man who made it, Trina. Only who the craftsman was—the artist who both blew the Chalice itself and then made that exquisite decoration on it.'

'The same man?' Trina marvelled, and he nodded.

'Yes. A man who lived for glass—and died by it. His name was Tyzak—Andrew Tyzak. And he was my great-grandfather.'

Trina sat bolt upright. Somehow, she found, she'd got herself on to Griff's lap, but just at the moment that wasn't important. 'Your *great-grandfather*?' she gasped.

'That's right. Just as Joshua Compson was yours. They worked together in those early days. It makes sense, Trina, if you think about it. Old Joshua wasn't a glass man, was he?—he took the factory over from some cousin who'd made a mess of it. But he himself was an ironmaster. So he must have had some craftsmen to start off with, and Andrew Tyzak was one of them. He made that Chalice and it became the family heirloom.'

'But why? Why *my* family's heirloom? What happened to Andrew—and why didn't he make any more? Why don't people *know* about him? I didn't.' A thought struck her. 'Did Dad know?'

'Yes, he knew, but only as a story at first, passed down by word of mouth. He knew that Joshua and Andrew Tyzak had been close friends and that they had great plans for the factory. They were going to do it all together. The Chalice, one of the first major pieces made, was proof of that. I suppose that's why Joshua kept it.'

'What happened?' Trina breathed, her eyes on the shadowed, haunted face. 'Something happened—what was it?'

'An accident in the glasshouse. An apprentice trying to be clever—someone tripping over, nobody really knows. But the gatherer had just collected a new iron. ... It was to be a large bowl, so there was a lot of metal on the end. ... It hit Andrew square on the head.'

Trina shuddered. Accidents in the glasshouse were rare and she had never heard of anything but the most minor of injuries being caused by molten glass while her father had been alive. But she could imagine the scene as the great mass of red-hot metal struck the glassmaker on the head. ... There would have been no chance, no chance at all.

'Oh, Griff,' she whispered, 'how horrible!'

'Yes. His wife never got over it. She left the area and went to Wales, taking her son with her—the son Andrew had hoped would take over his place in the factory—as craftsman and part-owner.' He glanced down at Trina. 'The documents had been drawn up for Joshua and Andrew to go into partnership. They were to have been signed the next day.'

Trina was silent, trying to take it all in. Griff's great-grandfather, making that beautiful Chalice which had always, to her, symbolised Compson's Crystal. ... the accident, killing its maker before he had time to do more. ... the partnership agreement that had never been signed. ...

'And did Dad know all that?' she asked at last.

'Yes. He found the documents in an old diary. Joshua had kept a record of everything that had happened. It had obviously broken his heart—the two men had made all their plans together and now all he had left was this one piece of glass—the Chalice. He'd tried to persuade Andrew's wife to let him have her son, to train him and take him into partnership, but she refused. And he had his own son, of course, but there was evidently a very close bond between him and Andrew.'

'And is that why Dad——'

'Your father determined to find if there were any Tyzaks left after he found those documents. He traced us—still in Wales, that's why I'm called Griffith. It was my mother's maiden name—Tyzak was altogether too outlandish, in her opinion! Anyway, your father found us and he offered me the chance of an apprenticeship if I wanted it.'

'And you did? But how did you know you wanted to work with glass? You'd been away from it—your father and grandfather had been away from it——'

'Yes, but my father was an artist in another way. He was badly hurt in the last war and he became a potter. There's not really that much difference between working with glass and working with clay, you know, and I was already showing some talent. The idea of glass excited me—and I wanted to do well. I wanted to be able to look after my parents as they grew older.'

'So that's why Compson's wasn't enough. You had to branch out.'

'Partly, and partly because your father actually wanted me to. Yet, in a way I believe he was disappointed—he'd set so much store on my coming into the firm later on. But he saw that I needed freedom to experiment and find my own level, and he encouraged me to go.'

That was more or less what Trevor had said. Trina looked up, half shyly, and said: 'So you didn't really betray him. And that's why he wanted you to come back.'

'That's why,' said Griff, and bent his head to hers.

Trina felt his lips, soft yet inexorable as they parted her own. His arms held her close; the hardness had gone from them and they cradled her as they might a baby; she nestled closer and sighed with pleasure as his hands found the opening of her dressing-gown and slipped inside.

'Shall we go back to square one?' he murmured against her ear. 'Or whatever square we were on that night in the sitting-room? Remember? Or maybe we need some more champagne. . . .'

'I don't need any champagne,' Trina whispered. She wasn't quite sure how it had happened, but all her hostility had melted and this time she knew it wouldn't return. She'd been wrong about Griff all along. He wasn't an opportunist, out to grab her family's firm. By rights, it should have been *his* family's firm too, and he would have come quite naturally into the position of part-owner. And the skill, the talent he displayed wasn't just a fluke—it had come down to him from the ancient glassmakers of Lorraine whose name he bore, down through the hands of the man who had made that beautiful Chalice. . . .

And that other piece of glass—the piece he himself had made, the glass sculpture that symbolised freedom in crystal—was it to mark a new era in the firm's history? Did he intend that it should become known as Compson Crystal, or was it to take the name of his own studio, Tyzak?

'What do you think, Trina?' he asked, twisting her question. 'You believe very strongly in this idea that beauty must be functional too, don't you?'

'Well——' she hesitated. 'Yes, I do. It's what we've always done. But I *can* see that it's lovely, Griff, and if you want——'

'Let me just say this,' he interrupted. 'Don't you think that beauty has a function of its own? You felt comforted when you held it in your hands. Isn't *that* function enough? You enjoyed looking at it—doesn't *that* suffice? Do you have to be able to put something in it as well? Come to that——' he glanced down at her with glinting eyes, '—how long is it since you've actually *used* that Chalice? Would you really call that functional too?'

Trina laughed and felt helpless. 'You'll always win

an argument!' she exclaimed. 'So what do you suggest?'

'That we use the Herefordshire studio for experimental work. That any of the men here who want to go and learn other things there, should go. That we try the glass—it already does have a market, after all—and see how it goes. If we need to expand—well, we can do it as and when necessary. We'll have the men and the equipment. And we can try colour in the same way, bringing it here only when it's proved itself. How does that strike you?'

'It seems such an obvious solution, I wonder why we never considered it before,' said Trina.

'Because we were both too damned obstinate,' he answered. 'You got across me with your suspicions and I made up my mind that I hadn't worked hard for over twenty years to be ordered about by a chit of a girl barely out of art college. There was so much I could see, coming in from the outside, and it seemed to me that you'd deliberately blinkered yourself to the truth. And when you started behaving as if I was out to wreck everything—well, I saw red. I just went ahead as I thought best, determined not to refer to you any more than I absolutely had to.' He grinned suddenly. 'What made it all the worse was the way I seemed to turn to jelly every time you appeared. I just wanted to take you in my arms and kiss you, especially when you got angry—and that made *me* all the angrier! I'd never planned on being undermined in that particular way—I always prided myself on being able to keep things strictly under control.'

'Like Julia?' Trina suggested slyly, and he snorted.

'Julia was a help to me when I first began, and that's all. I saw nothing of her until she discovered I'd come into Compson Crystal. Then she saw a chance of getting into something really big. I had to play along with her a bit—until I'd paid her back every penny of her part in my studio—but once that was done I was glad to say goodbye.'

Trina snuggled deeper into his arms. How stupid

hey'd both been! She, too, had been afraid of her own reactions to Griff. Confused about her father's reasons for bringing him in, she'd resented his presence from the start. And the physical effect he had on her had frightened and alarmed her—and caused more resentment. It was a wonder they hadn't driven each other away completely.

'Your piece of glass,' she murmured, 'do you want it back? It's part of the Arabian order, isn't it?'

'It was,' he said, 'but now I've got other plans for it. I can make another piece for Mohammed. But this one—well, I thought it would be a good idea to keep it with the Chalice. Don't you agree? It seems to have come full circle then, from my great-grandfather to me.'

'Keep them together?' Trina said. 'Here?'

'Well, of course,' he answered, tightening his arms around her. 'This is where we're going to live, isn't it?'

The fire crackled suddenly and flared up, and Trina turned into Griff's arms as if she were coming home. There was no need to say more. Their understanding was complete now, as it would have been before if only they could have allowed it. And as their lips stopped talking and found other things to do and the delight of love raced through their blood, she forgot all the animosity that had been between them and knew that at last she had found the man who could lead her through life, treating her as his partner but giving her his strength when she needed it. She stretched her body in his arms and shivered with excitement as he ran one hand down the length of her, then pulled him close in a frenzy of desire that would not abate.

'What about that old-fashioned courtship?' he whispered against her skin. 'I don't want you to be disappointed, Trina.'

'I won't be disappointed,' she assured him as she sought his body with fingers that were suddenly sure. 'We'll have that courtship, Griff. I don't want to miss a moment of it.' And as their clothes fell away at last and left them close and entwined in the glowing firelight, she added: 'We'll start tomorrow. . . .'

4 FREE
Harlequin Romances

Get all the latest books before they're sold out!

As a Harlequin subscriber you actually receive your personal copies of the latest Romances immediately after they come off the press, so you're sure of getting all 6 each month.

Cancel your subscription whenever you wish!

You don't have to buy any minimum number of books. Whenever you decide to stop your subscription just let us know and we'll cancel all further shipments.

Your FREE gift includes
- MAN OF POWER by **Mary Wibberley**
- THE WINDS OF WINTER by **Sandra Field**
- THE LEO MAN by **Rebecca Stratton**
- LOVE BEYOND REASON by **Karen van der Zee**

FREE GIFT CERTIFICATE
and Subscription Reservation
Mail this coupon today!

Harlequin Reader Service

In the U.S.A.
2504 West Southern Ave.
Tempe, AZ 85282

In Canada
P.O. Box 2800, Postal Station A
5170 Yonge Street,
Willowdale, Ont. M2N 5T5

Please send me my 4 Harlequin Romance novels FREE.
Also, reserve a subscription to the 6 NEW Harlequin
Romance novels published each month. Each month I will
receive 6 NEW Romance novels at the low price of $1.50
each (*Total–$9.00 a month*). There are no shipping and
handling or any other hidden charges. I may cancel this
arrangement at any time, but even if I do, these first 4 books
are still mine to keep. **116 BPR EASR**

NAME   (PLEASE PRINT)

ADDRESS   APT. NO.

CITY

STATE/PROV.   ZIP/POSTAL CODE

Offer not valid to present subscribers
Offer expires March 31, 1985

R-SUB-4X

If price changes are necessary you will be notified.

Harlequin reaches
into the hearts and minds
of women across America
to bring you

Harlequin American Romance™

YOURS FREE!

Enter a uniquely exciting new world with

Harlequin American Romance ™·

Harlequin American Romances are the first romances to explore today's love relationships. These compelling novels reach into the hearts and minds of women across America... probing the most intimate moments of romance, love and desire.

You'll follow romantic heroines and irresistible men as they boldly face confusing choices. Career first, love later? Love without marriage? Long-distance relationships? All the experiences that make love real are captured in the tender, loving pages of **Harlequin American Romances**.

What makes American women so different when it comes to love? Find out with **Harlequin American Romance!**

Send for your introductory FREE book now!

Get this book FREE!

Mail to:

Harlequin Reader Service

In the U.S.	In Canada
2504 West Southern Ave.	P.O. Box 2800, Postal Station A
Tempe, AZ 85282	5170 Yonge St., Willowdale, Ont. M2N 5T5

YES! I want to be one of the first to discover

Harlequin American Romance. Send me FREE and without obligation *Twice in a Lifetime.* If you do not hear from me after I have examined my FREE book, please send me the 4 new **Harlequin American Romances** each month as soon as they come off the presses. I understand that I will be billed only $2.25 for each book (total $9.00). There are no shipping or handling charges. There is no minimum number of books that I have to purchase. In fact, I may cancel this arrangement at any time. *Twice in a Lifetime* is mine to keep as a FREE gift, even if I do not buy any additional books. 154 BPA NAV4

Name _____ (please print)

Address _____ Apt. no.

City _____ State/Prov. _____ Zip/Postal Code

Signature (If under 18, parent or guardian must sign.)

AMR-SUB-3